More Than One Life

Miloslava Holubová

More Than One Life

Translated from the Czech
by Alex Zucker
with Lyn Coffin and Zdenka Brodská

NORTHWESTERN UNIVERSITY PRESS
Evanston, Illinois

Hydra Books
Northwestern University Press
Evanston, Illinois 60208-4210

Originally published in Czech in 1994 under the title *Víc než jeden život* by Melantrich, Prague. Copyright © 1994 by Miloslava Holubová. English translation copyright © 1999 by Hydra Books/Northwestern University Press. Published 1999.

Printed in the United States of America

ISBN 0-8101-1705-3

Library of Congress Cataloging-in-Publication Data

Holubová, Miloslava, 1913–
  [Víc než jeden život. English]
  More than one life/Miloslava Holubová; translated from the Czech by Alex Zucker, with Lyn Coffin and Zdenka Brodská.
    p. cm.
    "Hydra books."
    ISBN 0-8101-1705-3 (cloth : alk. paper)
    1. Children of divorced parents Fiction 2. Family Fiction. I. Zucker, Alex. II. Coffin, Lyn. III. Brodská, Zdenka. IV. Title.
PG5039.18.O44V5313 1999
891.8'6354—DC21   99-13058
                                                       CIP

More Than One Life

I nearly said hello.

When I first noticed him, he walked using a cane, though still fully upright. Later on, his gait deteriorated. Occasionally I would see him on my way to work: As I hurried along the square, I would pass him struggling uphill in the opposite direction, each time stooping more than the last. But when he took his seat in the doctor's waiting room, he always held himself erect. He was tall and thin, with a gray goatee—he had probably had it forever; he didn't look like the type to follow fashion—and a pair of glasses perched atop a nice, full nose. Whenever Aunt Klára evaluated the men in our family, she described our dad as having the nose of a pharaoh crossed with an American Indian. That was just the sort of nose the elderly gentleman had.

Sometimes I wouldn't see him at all for long periods, and then nearly every day, when he came to the clinic for shots. He always brought along his German shepherd, and when they got to the clinic door he would stop and say: "I'm sorry, but you can't come in with me. Just wait here, all right?" Then he would give the dog a pat and let him off his leash.

The dog would wait patiently in the hallway, his handsome looks drawing the attention of patients and tenants alike. Although he didn't discriminate when it came to children, he was always particular about which adults he allowed to pet him. He would watch carefully, and if anyone dared to reach out a hand, he would emphatically take a step back—to the embarrassment of many, including myself.

"So," I said, "not good enough for you, am I? That's a shame, because I like you, and your master too." And the dog came closer, and became warm and friendly.

I made the dog's acquaintance first. It took a long time before I was brave enough to approach the elderly gentleman, so I just went on watching. Sometimes I would pass the two of them on the street or on Kampa and overhear the man talking softly to the dog. In time I came to recognize them even from a distance. When his master spoke, the dog would respond with his tail and ears, often turning his head to listen as he padded alongside. In between he would go scampering off, but he was always quick to return so that he could report on where he had been and what he had seen. Sometimes his master would give him advice on what to visit—"How about Čertovka, is the brook frozen over yet, are there children out on it?"—and the dog would eagerly run off to investigate and then return, exultant, once again.

One day some friends of mine lent me their children and I took them out for a riverboat ride on the Vltava. It was an early autumn afternoon and still chilly enough that Střelecký Island was deserted. But then suddenly I spotted the man and his dog sitting on a park bench, their backs to the river. They looked like one of those old married couples, the two of them seated so close together it was as if they were attached. To this day I can still see their backs. They appeared to be simply staring straight ahead, engaged in quiet conversation, when all at once the dog sprang to the alert, pricking up his ears. He swiveled his head back and forth several times, first to his master and then straight ahead; then he lifted his head, barked a few times, looked at the ground, and back up and down again—all in a state of extreme agitation. I drew it to the children's attention, and we too became upset. What was going on? Had he lost something? After a brief debate, we decided the elderly gentleman was probably just pointing out one of the branches swaying in the breeze and the shadows it cast on the ground in front of them.

I must have caught cold on that outing, because not long afterward my slipped disc began acting up dreadfully. And evidently the elderly gentleman ought not to have been sitting out on that bench either, because we both ended up going for shots for some time after the incident.

One day as the nurse was giving me my injection, the elderly gentleman was with Dr. Jílková in the next room and the door was open just a crack. "Next time you should send someone else to pick up your prescription so you won't have to climb that hill," I overheard the doctor say. But the elderly gentleman laughed: "Oh, I can still make it, and besides I don't have anyone."

I was struck by his tone of voice, admitting neither pity nor concern. Really? I wondered. Why is that? Did they all die on you? Did they leave the country? Or have they just forgotten you? You live all on your own? I can't believe it. You mean you never had a wife, not even before the war? I'll bet you were a looker, and judging from the silver cane handle, elegant ring, and sophisticated if well-worn suit, a wealthy man, too.

No, this was not some old retiree sitting on a park bench recounting everything about himself from five generations back. Quite the contrary. He was the sort whom others confided in while he sat, legs crossed, hands clasped over his cane handle, staring solemnly into the distance, so it was as though he didn't exist, as though he were only an ear, a horn on an antique phonograph. And as that ear vibrated, the nostrils quivered also in sympathy, and in that manner, without a word, the old gentleman would respond with active yet unobtrusive concern to each sentence uttered.

I'm a sociable, talkative person. I would be all too happy to confide in someone. But who? Who would want to know and who would understand the long, tangled history that chafes at every edge of my soul?

After more than four hours of passionate debate—about

5

fifteen of us were over at Eva's—I was tired; I lost track of the conversation, and after drifting around the room a while, my eyes dropped anchor at the Biedermeier cabinet I had loaned to Eva years earlier because it didn't fit in with our new apartment. I noticed it on every visit, but now all of a sudden it was like running into a relative in a foreign city.

I can't believe it, what brings you here? It's so nice to see you! Hello, hello, my compliments, old girl. We've known each other for years, but you still look as marvelous as ever. I see you've got new curtains: pretty. You only grow more beautiful with age, I suppose, just so long as no one does you any damage. And my goodness, that color of yours! That gorgeous yellow golden brown with a touch of red! I wonder, where did the cherry tree from which they made you grow?

It must have bloomed sometime in the days of Julien Sorel and Eugene Onegin; Napoleon himself may have slowed his horse down a step to pluck one of your blossoming branches after the Battle of Austerlitz. Except that was in December, so that can't be. Perhaps then it was one of his dashing officers, nursing his wounds till spring when he fell in love and inhaled your fragrance in a state of infatuation. Naturally you, my dear cabinet, were still but a glimmer in the carpenter's eye. And who knows how many months your timber still had to rest and ripen before he could set to work?

What is it, what's wrong? Are you homesick?

And yet you're so pretty—those graceful legs, those deep-bottomed drawers—oh, how well I know them!

And now you've got chestnut trees outside the window again, their green magic dancing across your glass.

And who was it that made those brass rings in the lions' mouths on the drawers? Probably some master metalsmith like our great-great-uncle Francek (the scoundrel who, spent after a bender, hid in a confessional during high mass and, after sleepily accepting an old granny's confession, did penance by walking to Rome, while his faithful wife, Apolenka, looked after the shop and their half-dozen children).

Who was that sighing, you or me? I suppose you wonder why you're here and you blame me somewhat for it, don't you?

How many of my ancestors' hands have touched you? They would have stored linen in your drawers, or perhaps doilies and tablecloths, since the shelves up above behind the glass were for china, a coffee set for special occasions most likely.

Silent witness, humble servant, you won't say a thing, I know, dear cabinet. But the going must have been rough in those days, as it was in the next ones and the next. Doubtless you were moved under some highly irregular circumstances, although entire years may have passed with nothing more dramatic than a slightly burned cake served on the cut-glass dish alongside the coffee cups.

I didn't know you as part of the family until you stood in Dad's room. That was around the time when our parents stopped using the big master bedroom because they said they had trouble sleeping in there. I remember how flattered I was when Mom consulted me on what to put in Dad's room. It was the quietest room in the house, right off the garden, beautiful beyond question. But when she and I showed him what we had done—a vase of cream-colored roses on the little table between the windows, beneath a watercolor by Mánes—he merely remarked that it seemed somehow sad. Then, noticing my disappointment, he hastened to add that it was probably just his imagination.

"It's getting dark out," he said. "All it needs is a little brightening up." He kept looking around the room until he spotted the cabinet. For some reason it bothered me that he was standing with his back to Mom, so I quickly stuttered out a few words and he turned to face us. He complimented us on the pleasant color scheme—the café au lait curtains, the soft pastel-brown Persian rug, the olive bedspread—and gave Mom a look, probably thinking: All these peaceful colors are supposed to calm my nerves. She must have read that somewhere, or perhaps the doctor suggested it. My favorite is red, but of course I'm not allowed to have that.

I wanted to leave but couldn't bring myself to walk through the space between my mom and dad—it was as if there were a mesh of live wires between them, woven out of their nerves—so I crawled under the table by the wall where Mom was standing.

"What on earth are you doing? You act like you're still a baby," she said, and the two of them burst out laughing.

One night just before bedtime, I went to see my dad in his room. As usual, however, the conversation faltered, so I sat down in the armchair by the cabinet and awkwardly played with the rings on the drawers.

"It is a nice cabinet, isn't it?"

"Yes, I like it."

"Me too. We used to have it in the dining room when we lived at the mill, and now here it is with me. Whenever I can't fall asleep, I sit up and talk to the cabinet about the way things used to be back home and the way things are now."

"How come grown-ups have trouble sleeping?"

"Well, not all grown-ups have trouble sleeping. It depends. But I think it's time for you to go beddy-bye. Run along now, the governess must be looking for you."

As the baby of the family, arriving nine years behind his siblings, my dad slept in his parents' room. In winter, so they would have more air, they kept the bedroom windows shut and left the door to the dining room open. Lying there in his little bed, the boy would peer up at the cabinet, especially the rings in the lions' mouths, which he had used to hold himself up as a toddler, just as his brothers and sisters and father had before him.

One Saturday night, after taking his bath—as the youngest in the family, he always went first—he climbed into bed all squeaky clean and nestled into the comforters up to his nose. But as he drifted off to sleep, from under his drooping eyelids he caught a glimpse of the rings in the lions' mouths glistening like gold in the room next door. But it was dark out! How could that be? What was going on? And he sat right up and took a look around.

Down to earth and into the dining room, the full moon beamed out its light, the hushed decibels of desire that have stirred every living creature since time immemorial.

It drew the boy out of bed, too. First he went to touch the rings in the lions' mouths and then he walked to the window. It had started to snow at the beginning of the week. Not much, just enough to coat the landscape with frosting. The temperature hadn't dropped to freezing yet, the snow was barely holding on, but then suddenly it had stopped snowing and a big freeze set in, so that everywhere you looked it was white. But the mill pond had frozen overnight, and now it was sparkling, dark and fantastic, in the moonlight.

You couldn't have found a better slide in Paradise itself!

The boy stared, transfixed. He wasn't the only one to fall under the spell, however. Perched on his hind legs on the pond's snowy edge was their black dog, Rex, snout upturned, barking and whining as if in song.

In the whole white world it was just the three of them: moon, dog, and boy. Everyone else was on some other planet, hastily finishing the evening chores and lining up for the bathtub.

All at once the boy tore himself away from the window and scampered as is, barefoot in his floppy white nightshirt, out of the room, down the stairs, across the yard, and out to the pond. He gave Rex a brief hello, then hop! sprang onto the smooth expanse of dark, shining ice. Crouching down nice and low on landing so as not to lose his balance, he made it as far as the middle of the pond before sliding to a stop. At first the dark gleam made Rex uneasy, but within a second he had joined the boy, licking at him as he ran alongside. When the boy stood back up, the soles of his feet stung so badly he hopped around groaning, "Ow, ow!" But he couldn't help it, it was as though he were possessed, and again hop! and again that heavenly slide, with the huffing and puffing Rex at his side.

Later that night, his mom went to peek in on her darling son and found him lovingly embracing the furry Rex beneath the striped comforters. The boy didn't even stir at her startled cry, and Rex just wagged his tail under the covers, then vanished like a shadow.

I assume the story had a happy ending, because Dad had no unpleasant memories of the incident, and he cherished the delight of that evening all his life.

"You know, children, today it seems strange that sliding was all I could think of, and yet I managed to see and take in so much. I can remember the freshly scrubbed stairs, the clean-swept yard, the grass still visible beneath the light snow, the white willow trees alongside the pond, and beyond it the meadow climbing up to the woods. And what I couldn't see, I knew and sensed: the carp below the ice, the squirrels, the deer, the rabbits in the woods, the bats in the attic, the chickens in the henhouse, the geese, the pigs, the sheep, the cows in the barn, the horses in the stable, and my momma and poppa and brothers and sisters in the warm, snow-covered house. I was aware of all that existed back there in the mill behind me, but everything here as well—above and below the ice, and in and around the woods, the grand music of silence, and touching it all was the light of the moon, and the light was like a living thing."

Dad's "heavenly moonlight slide," as it came to be called in his countless retellings, has become our inalienable birthright, and it is now being passed on to the next generations.

But what do Mojmír's children in Canada think when they hear it, or Libuše's grandchildren in Rome? Those who have at least some memories of Grandpa and what we shared, and those who grew up far away from our family and all that was ours?

Some time later the cabinet was put in my room. By then it was known as the laundry chest, owing to Dad's use of the drawers for socks and underwear. I myself used it for all sorts of things but kept the laundry up on the shelves with the glass doors; that was probably when the cabinet got its first curtains, so you couldn't see inside. Dad had kept books up there.

After I got married, I put the cabinet–cum–laundry chest in our bedroom. I would lie in bed and look at it, and when insomnia struck me also, I too began to talk to it.

So what secrets did Dad tell you? He complained about Mom and us, didn't he? Come on, you can tell me — on second thought, never mind, I've had enough of that already. All I want to know is, what do you do when your life doesn't work out the way you want it to? Surely by now you must have seen and heard it all; you've got experience. So don't just sit there, give me some advice!

When they locked me up, the only thing that Dad brought back to his place from my apartment was the old cabinet. Then, after my release, I put it in the kitchen next to the sink. It was an ugly apartment, but I tried to make it livable.

I didn't talk to the cabinet anymore, and I had completely forgotten about our former nighttime conversations. For one thing, despite all my trials and tribulations, things were getting better; and for another, although I am ashamed to admit it, I was happy. I only spoke to the cabinet once, when we were hammering nails for a towel rack into her comely side (the one facing the sink, which was hidden by a curtain). I apologized, patting the cabinet like a loyal horse: "Sorry, old girl, I know I shouldn't do this, but we live in turbulent times, you know. And besides, the more useful you are, the longer you'll be here with us. So tra-la-la-la-la, come on now, smile!"

Several years later I spotted a group of Americans at the Hermitage in Leningrad. They were examining a silver-plated door inlaid with tortoiseshell and pointing to an ugly tin strip with the inventory number attached to the work of art by a common nail. "I can understand," I said in English, but with a smile different from theirs. "In eventful times, all kinds of things are done 'temporarily' and then stay that way for a very long time." The Americans silently walked away.

But now it occurs to me: How was it, anyway, that you made the move from Dad's room to mine? We were living with Mom at Grandpa's, so it must have been after our parents got divorced. I can still see the shadows on your wood, the strange green reflections that flashed in your glass whenever a strong wind rocked the treetops outside the window. It's all so strange. I wonder how come Dad didn't keep you? He rescued you in the fifties, while I was in prison, which proves that he truly loved you.

At the time of the family disaster, all of us children were angry with Dad because he was the one who asked for the divorce and made Mom leave the house. ("My house," he called it, and yet it belonged to both of them.) She was seriously ill, so it seemed obvious to us that we should take her side.

I still don't how the cabinet ended up with me. Either my dad offered it to me and I didn't even notice that he was trying to do something nice—I barely thanked him, probably a nod and that was it; or else he was so downtrodden and bitter that he was already thinking of suicide. I just don't know. But however it happened, I'm afraid that I exhibited a sizable measure of rudeness and insensitivity. Whether I accepted the cabinet only because it was convenient—in terms of size, perhaps, or color—without any thought to how much it meant to him; or whether he himself didn't want it—our childhood years, both his and mine, were ancient history; either way, it still upsets me to remember it.

"Daddy, tell us what it was like when you were little," we

would plead, and he was more than happy to talk. Of course that was when we were children. We loved him then. But when did we stop, and why?

"I know that you all find me boring and offensive. Do you think I don't notice how you avoid me? The way you disappear after dinner to study, and then when it's time for bed the governess finds you over at the caretaker's house."

He was right. It was always peaceful there. Mrs. Bylinková was a sweet woman, and besides, it was fun with Mr. Bylinka. They had a tomcat, and their son, Toník, went to school with us. We always tried to sneak up the stairs unnoticed when we came home, but our four pairs of scampering feet and whispered warnings—"Shhh, shhh, quiet!"—were louder than we thought. The door to the study would fly open, and Dad would lean out into the hall and yell, livid with rage, his deep, booming voice echoing down the stairs, pinning us where we stood.

Then sometimes Mom would come to the rescue. Suddenly the piano in the sunroom would stop short, and she would appear, pale and quiet, at the other end of the hall. "Please, Matouš, take it easy," she would say softly, solemnly, admonishingly. And Dad would disappear into his study. But sometimes afterward—and that was the worst—he would guiltily creep upstairs to apologize, explaining that our lack of love for him was due to a tremendous beating that none of us could remember. We dismissed his colorful account, with embarrassing new details each time, as exaggerated if not outright invented.

Eventually our mom confirmed that there had in fact been a beating and that it had truly been awful. She said that she had been afraid he would kill us, and went to fetch Mr. Bylinka (of course she rang for the maid to fetch him; she wouldn't have left us alone). Everyone was there—the governess, the cook, the maid, the caretaker—my God! All four of us ended up coming down with a high fever. But Mom wouldn't tell us the whole story until we were adults, long after Dad had moved out of the house. When we were children, she always just changed the subject.

Dad went on being high-strung, but he never so much as laid a hand on us after that. Once his screaming ceased to terrify us, it was simply annoying. So far as we were concerned, that horrible beating had been nothing but a feverish nightmare.

Yes, a feverish nightmare. That must have been Mom's idea. I can hear her now, dismissing our childish questions with a smile: "Why, of course not, he never did anything of the sort. You were only sick with fever, and delirious. But you're well again now, and it's a sunny day!" Even if it wasn't, rain, sleet, or snow, she always managed to look on the bright side. "Now just go to sleep and clear all those nasty dreams from your heads!" The younger children accepted her interpretation as a matter of course, and the older ones were happy to do the same. Our mom's insistence convinced us that we were incapable of distinguishing dream from reality; that and the fact that, somewhere deep down, we loved our dad—although we came to forget that in the years to come.

After all, how could we not remember such a beating? The oldest one of us, at least, must have in school by then, right? But even that we can't be sure of, since we accepted our mom's story without question and never returned to the subject again, and now there is no one left to ask.

What was it like for our dad, though? To see those four little bodies—his own children!—shaking with delirious fever? Mom didn't blame him, but the unspeakable guilt he felt nevertheless must have been nerve-racking.

And what brought him to such a state? Why is it that no one ever talked about it?

We faulted him for being selfish (only in our minds or among ourselves at first, but eventually to his face), for always dwelling on his own troubles and not talking about anything but himself over and over. Because as hard as he hammered home how much he loved us, he still had to look in a notebook to see how old we were and which grade we were in (at least he didn't mix up our names—but he did!—oh, come on, don't try to tell me he didn't know what our names were!). And when he was in a sentimental mood and lifted one of us up on his lap, kind and gentle, saying, "So tell me something about yourself," before we could even finish a sentence, he would interrupt: "Oh, I know what that's like, oh boy, when I was your age . . . ," and once again we would have to sit and listen to him talk about himself.

Yes, all that was true, but after listening to him explain for the tenth or eleventh time that the reason we had stopped loving him was because of that beating, after which he would forgive us because he felt guilty, we would mumble an obligatory "Of course we love you! We don't remember that at all!" How come we always looked down at the ground when we said it? How come we didn't wrap our arms around his neck and just ask, at least once: "So what made you do it?"

We couldn't ask. It was too upsetting. We didn't want to imagine him beating small children like a madman—and maybe Mom as well, when she tried to protect us. The less we talked about it, the more we felt that his rage sprang from some sad secret between him and Mom. That was what we feared, and it hovered over us like a dark cloud all through our childhood.

Mom never even mentioned the secret until we were grown-ups, and even then very little. Still, I don't recall her ever telling us, "You're just children, mind your own business. Wait until you get older." She might have; but there was probably no need. For instance, the time we were having lunch and Dad started screaming that the soup was too salty, or not salty enough, and he hurled the bowl to the floor and Mom softly ordered us upstairs. So we ran off, hearing his furious voice all the way up the stairs until the governess closed the door behind us. Later Mom came up to see us, looking tired but steady. She asked how we were doing in school, and no one said a word about what had happened. We felt good with her, safe. With Mom around, the menacing cloud that haunted us even in sleep was nowhere to be seen.

Dad was incapable of that kind of self-discipline. He was convinced that whenever we were with Mom she would complain about him, slander him, try to turn us against him. So whenever he got us alone, he would justify and boast and accuse us and Mom of one thing or another, constantly summoning up that fearsome cloud. We were never safe with him; he would start screaming furiously out of the blue, or torment us with nonsense about Mom—and if we stood up for her, we ended up screaming, too. So we avoided him whenever possible, and when there was no way around it we were so careful to avoid the subject that we would become tangled up in a snarl of confusion, doubt, and fear, and not know what to talk about at all.

What is a man to do when he's alone in his own family? The hawk tells his woes to his own kind, they say, and so Dad told his woes to the cabinet.

Huddled and weeping, I am underneath the piano in the corner of the parlor at our grandparents' house. I raise my head to look, as many feet engaged in giddy conversation make their way in from the hall, and notice my brother Mojmír right next to me, hiding under the same piano—could he be crying too? We are both embarrassed, but there is no time to be ashamed, because the sofa and armchairs on the other side of the room, where the company will be sitting, afford a wonderful view of the piano. It's time for a vanishing act, and fast. I'm closest to the door, so I go first.

Something bad had happened at home again before we left for Grandpa and Grandma's, and sitting in the carriage across from our parents was not the best way to forget it.

Another time I caught Libuše by surprise in the thick

hedges along the garden wall, where we used to hide in times of trouble. We huddled together, arms clutched around each other's shoulders, watching with tears streaming down our faces as the guests settled in at the tables on the patio. All of the laughter and cheerful shouts! And no one but the children hidden in the jasmine noticed our parents' forced smiles and mournful eyes.

Years later, during a visit to some friends, Libuše and I went to take a walk through the June garden. We stopped at a blossoming bush of jasmine and stood there a while talking. My sister broke off a twig, lifted it over her head, and turned it over, chatting away as she studied the underside of the leaves and blossoms.

"Do you realize what you're doing?" I said, laughing. She looked up, surprised. "I only meant that I do the same. Jasmine in bloom always reminds me of how we used to meet crying our eyes out in the bushes." We looked at each other, then Libuše nodded, smiled, and we hugged.

So why was it that we didn't go to Mom with our pain, as we did with everything else? We felt bad for both of them, I think, and there were times when we didn't want to go to just one—and that means we loved them both. What Dad would have given for a sign of love like that!

Every time we visited him after he moved out, he would bring up "our problem." And we of course would stubbornly dodge and sidestep, keeping our mouths shut. He would go right on justifying and blaming, while we turned a deaf ear and waited distractedly for him to finish. He noticed, he could sense it, obviously, and it became almost a matter of life and death for him (but it was, it really was!), but he just went on ranting and raving, not wanting to stop, not able to stop, and then he would raise his voice and start to scream—there he goes again!—turning meaner and meaner by the minute, and we were too, until all of us felt sick to our stomachs and he was too drained to go on; after all, he was getting old. Then, eyes closed, he would fall back breathless in his chair, wishing he could die—and not one of us gave him so much as a pat on the back.

My brother Mojmír comes to mind. For thirty years now, he says, he has been peacefully at war with his wife. He even considered divorce, but then Helena said she loved him and begged him to stay. "Love me?" Mojmír said, amazed. "I was ready to leave because I was tired of not knowing whether you loved me or not. Usually I feel that I'm just getting on your nerves and bringing you down, that you're not happy with me."

As I recall, Mojmír didn't want to get married. God knows how it ever happened, but I do know that he didn't regret it afterward—in fact, he said that he only truly fell in love with Helena after they were married. Still—and it only occurs to me now, as I look at the cabinet; Mojmír probably hasn't thought of it yet—how many times has he hurt her, insulted her, humiliated her, frozen her feelings of warmth with neglect? And now Helena is not unlike Mojmír with Dad, knowing and feeling how he suffers as he waits for a single loving word. Mojmír wanted so badly to help, but couldn't manage those three words, or even a gesture requiring no words at all. It was all there inside of him, reserved for Dad alone, and even though he ached with the same pain as Dad, he couldn't bring himself to do it. . . .

It's strange: I finally took a look at the holes the nails left in the side of the cabinet, and it truly is amazing how little they are. I suppose that wood's wounds heal faster than ours.

It all comes rushing in on me, as if someone had taken everything ever contained in the cabinet's drawers and shelves and dumped it out over my head, and now it's scattered everywhere and I'm sitting in the middle of the floor trying to make some sense out of it.

This is what I see on my first run-through.

We closed our eyes and were sucked into the misery. In our confusion we turned selfish, standing up only for our right to peace and quiet. And now that we are beginning to understand and figure things out, it's too late. But then again, maybe not. For history is the teacher of life in all things, great and small.

How many times did we listen to Dad thunder in that fire-and-brimstone voice which so unnerved us: "To hell with it all, I don't care about any of it. I just want to give you my experience, do you hear? My *experience!*" And we thought: What on earth is he so riled up for if he doesn't give a damn?

We failed to grasp that by "experience" he meant the knowledge he had gained through a mountain of suffering. That was what he wanted to spare us.

I also used to see the elderly gentleman at the dairy market under the arcade and in the produce store on Market Square—there I had an especially good opportunity to observe him. It was best when he was standing in line on one side of the counter and I was on the other side, facing the opposite direction, so I could look him square in the face.

Sometimes he would shamble along so lost in thought he didn't seem to see anything around him, filling his basket with fruit and vegetables without even realizing it. Then, when it would come time to pay, he would look up in surprise—"Oh, of course"—and quickly fumble for his money. It was as though he had erected a sort of screen around himself so no one would take any notice of him. If anything actually had happened and the police had questioned the other shoppers about a tall old man with a gray beard and glasses, they probably would have said they hadn't seen him. Yet whenever anyone would bump into him, or even just brush against him (I tried it once), he would lift his hat, bow slightly, and say, "Pardon me."

At other times he was almost outgoing, cupping a hand to his ear as he leaned over to listen to the short lady in front of him in line, greeting the saleswoman, and then eagerly turning his eye to the goods: the jams and jellies and canned vegetables on the shelves in front, the fresh vegetables in baskets along the wall. He would always stand there concentrating a while before carefully making his selection.

One day I entered the shop just as he stepped up to the

cash register. "Isn't it lovely, ma'am?" he said to the cashier, holding out a fresh green nest of broad, fleshy leaves with a carved ivory globe nestled in the middle.

I was picking up a basket on the other side of the counter when I heard him and saw the cauliflower. He was right; it was truly lovely. As I waited in line, I could picture my grandmother's vegetable patch, separated from the decorative garden by a low fence covered with clematis, the old gardener standing there in a sun-bleached blue smock, a sun-browned straw hat on his head. I strained to watch as he filled the basket in his wheelbarrow with cauliflower, kohlrabi, lettuce, and radishes. The sun beat down on my back, filling the air with the fragrance of honey, and somewhere nearby were Grandma and Grandpa, Mom and Dad, aunts and uncles and assorted children—no one was left alone.

Then I came to the counter—"Two heads of lettuce and one kilo of oranges, please"—and suddenly I could hear my own gray-haired father saying, "Look at that cauliflower, isn't it lovely?" And then, realizing that I failed to see any beauty in such a common vegetable, he just let out a sigh and smiled, "Well, never mind." After that we both were at pains not to spoil the rest of my brief visit.

When I arrived, I found him putting away groceries in the kitchen; he was living on his own at the time, and did all the housekeeping himself. After he showed me the cauliflower, I could tell he had to restrain himself from saying, "That's the foreign blood in you. If I were your mother, you would have appreciated it." Then again, perhaps he had other thoughts running through his mind; perhaps he was wondering: Why does that girl of mine keep her eyes closed so much?

Then came the eventful years around '68. It is beyond belief, truly beyond belief, how many things happened and how much my life—and not only mine—changed. Even today, more than ten years later, I sometimes wonder: Is this really my life? Am I still me? Perhaps there has been some incredible mistake. Perhaps I picked up the wrong coat from the cloakroom, for instance, and put on someone else's life. Perhaps I took a train in the wrong direction, or got off at the wrong stop and became hopelessly lost. And now I'm searching for my children, my husband, myself—the past, the present—feeling out the future with the help of a white cane.

When I next spotted the elderly gentleman, months later, it nearly broke my heart. His stoop was worse than ever, and he couldn't walk without stopping to rest every few minutes. And he was still alone, except for his dog. How many times, despite being in a hurry, had I stood there watching him, lost in thought, until he entered a shop or turned the corner? How do you manage to go on when you're so old and racked with pain?

He once brought down the house—I mean my dad again now—because the maid had made his bed wrong or put the pillowcase on inside out. "What is the meaning of this? How many times do I have to tell that silly goose?" Wild-eyed and livid with rage, he pounded the call button until the young maid appeared at his bedside, pale and weak in the knees. When he saw how terrified she was, he dismissed her with a wave of his hand—"Oh, never mind, run along"— and sank back in his bed, exhausted. Out in the hall, the cook clutched the maid by the hand—"What did I tell you?"—and then turned to the frightened little heads poking out of their bedroom doors: "Now back to bed, everything is fine. Your daddy is just upset again."

That was once upon a time, now it's water under the bridge. And then suddenly he was alone, with no one to talk to. Cast out of his own world, he washed up in some unfamiliar city: Prague, Brno, Bratislava—it didn't matter. He plunged into the gloomy depths of desolation. How could it have happened, the wrong, the injustice? For years he brooded, sleepless nights and delirious days twisting themselves into an impenetrable jungle seething with poisonous swamps.

How could it have happened?

He walked the city streets, killing time. Picking a tram at random, he would ride to the end of the line and take a walk. The next time he would ride a different line to the other end of town and walk along the river, through fields and forests. Wherever he went he felt only the depths of desolation, and yet he knew that somewhere up above was the normal world in which people went about their work, as he himself had done all his life—the world in which his wife and children lived and loved one another, chatting happily among themselves.

Dear brothers, this is a letter to Mojmír, but (thanks to carbon paper) I'm talking to you too, Václav, because behind your forbearing silence I sense more or less the same feeling. For two weeks now I have been debating you both in my mind, and for two days—I set Saturday as my deadline and today is Sunday—I have been racking my brains trying to figure out how to put it down on paper.

First of all, I am amazed at how many pages Mojmír, the notorious nonwriter, squandered in order to tell us that we were upsetting ourselves for no reason: "What large family doesn't have problems and conflicts between husband and wife and parents and children? What point is there in viewing it as the transference and continuation of destiny? And assuming there is such a thing as destiny, then how can you avoid it?"

You know, I have been staring at that phrase "the transference and continuation of destiny" for two weeks, wondering where you picked it up. It wasn't from me or Libuše, which proves that no matter how you try to escape, you are in it as deep as we are.

When a mother is separated from her children, she remains with them in spirit, her thoughts revolving constantly around the family circle; the poor woman can get so caught up that it becomes unhealthy. In the same way, you see our "tinkering" with the past as harmful. But it is more likely a sign of recovery—not a return to the past, but a process of self-discovery, a search for a way out of the blindness that has us trapped in a vicious circle.

Don't worry: Clearing things up can do Mom no harm. On the contrary, it can only confirm what a truly exceptional person she was. It is only to her credit if we find that she was right when she later reflected, "The poor man didn't have it easy with me either." By the time she said that, we were all over twenty, but we didn't give it much consideration; all we cared about was breaking her chain of thought so that we could change the subject.

Lest we forget, Mom was bone-tired and in love with her children. She may not have been strong enough to give us a truthful account of her difficulties with Dad, but at least she pointed our hearts and minds in the right direction. We were just too thick-skinned for it to sink in.

Sometimes, in a peaceful moment, she would suddenly sigh and say, "If only he weren't so agitated today." We would all just quickly change the subject, because we knew that Dad wasn't calm and never would be. As far as we were concerned, it was his fault; that was his nature, and we were glad he wasn't around, because he would only have made it hell for all of us.

And did it bother us that he *lived in hell? Not really. We were amazingly good at not thinking about it. How many wonderful evenings did we spend in one another's company, how many bright Sundays in cheery serenity? And if we (by which I mean we children) thought about him at all, it was only to reassure ourselves that with him around it would have been impossible.*

Without him, everything seemed easier, more relaxed.

Gone was the constant, exhausting stress of wondering, "What will it be today?" It wasn't until after Dad's departure that we came to know the peaceful intimacy of the family circle, the warmth of companionship, the effortless feeling of belonging.

Although we never said it aloud, we appreciated it especially after the war broke out. Imagine having to deal with him every day on top of the war! Eventually it sank in that he was alone, and we sent him some eggs and a roast pig, a callous act which we justified by pointing out that he was the one who had asked for the divorce, on account of his crazy escapade with the young lady, and he had only told Mom when she was seriously ill. A sixty-year-old man ought to know better. What did he expect after a stunt like that?

Today we are beyond such foolish questions. What he wanted was understanding. Before he died if possible; afterward if not. Each passing year since his death brings us closer to a more balanced perspective, a calm acceptance, as we hear a quiet voice in the distance calling out for justice.

Once you have given it some serious thought and you join us in our quest, you will be shocked to realize just how wrong we were. God knows how many mountains and valleys we must cross before we can even begin to understand. But the longer we fail to recognize our own guilt, the worse off we will be. In my mind, that is the most and the least we can do.

And yet it is no mean feat. The admission of guilt is not merely a onetime act. And nothing can be cleared up without us. Like metal submerged in a crucible, we are transformed, our vision shifts, and new questions arise as the unfortunate mess unravels. Sometimes change happens one step at a time, sometimes by leaps and bounds. And each new insight springs the lock on a secret door opening onto a new, brighter space, rinsed clean by the rain.

Yes, now I know. For years on end, we manage to brush off our painful thoughts as if they were so many pesky flies. We proudly patrol our wall of defense, constructed entirely of *self-deception, and at the first sign of the slightest crack we fill it in with cement and cover it over with reasoning. Anything that might upset our peace of mind or good spirits is promptly rejected, recast, reinterpreted, and resolutely forgotten. Forgotten and cast into the deepest dungeons along with whatever else burdens our heads and hearts—"Take it away!"—so we can go on stubbornly clinging to our belief that it isn't there and never has been.*

But when it comes time to search ourselves—and that time is never of our choosing—oh, how cruel it is. Shame, remorse, astonishment, all come crashing in at once. How could that have been me? How could I have been so wrong, so cruel, so heartless, so blind?!

For instance, the night the news of Mom's death arrived out of the blue.

In the midst of all the heartbreak and confusion, it was not sorrow or pain that I felt most, but rage—a rage purely like my dad's—at the evil trick that fate had played on me! Me! We had been counting so much on seeing each other again when she came back! I felt betrayed by life itself. No, no, no! I wanted just to howl and howl like an animal in the desert. I didn't want to see anyone, not even my own children; and as for him, the man who had caused my mother so much grief, not a chance.

That night was the only time in my life I ever sent my children away when they wanted to be with me. It was as if a safety valve inside me had blown and all of the suffering that had accumulated over the years erupted in raging sorrow, not just for the loss of Mom, but for our family, our country—everything! The irreplaceable loss, the absurdity of our mother dying in some foreign country—with still so much left unsolved, unspoken. What would we do, trapped here in our spell without her?

I realize now that I acted crazy out of spite, plunging myself into despair the same way Dad used to do whenever

is — with the children. How gentle her touch — with the children.

One day he found a newspaper clipping on her night table with an underlined poem: "I know a house with seven steps / They go from door to ground / And on the middle step sits pain / My friendly, faithful hound." So she too suffers. But she at least has the children. I have nothing. Nothing but sorrow and emptiness.

"Listen to this, Mommy."

"Go ahead, honey, I'm listening."

"Whenever I see Zdena and her daddy, they're always holding hands and talking and laughing. What do you think they talk about all the time?"

"Well, the same things as you and me, I suppose."

"Really?"

"There are a lot more journals where those came from. That black leather trunk was full of them. Remember how we used to climb inside it when we played hide-and-seek up in the attic?"

"How could I forget! But what happened to them? The journals, I mean?"

"Well, that was the time I ran into Václav on the stairs."

"I'm burning Dad's journals," he said. "I was just going up for more. What should I do with them?"

As we spoke, he opened the cracked black trunk to show me there was nothing left inside, and we both froze, startled at the sheer emptiness. The oriental pattern on the purple silk, also cracked in places, swam before our eyes.

I was about to give him a piece of my mind, but then I just stared into the emptiness and softly said: "How could they be in the way up in that great big attic?"

"Do you think anyone will ever read them?" Václav replied just as softly.

I didn't answer the question, and started marching upstairs. Václav walked beside me at first, then sprinted ahead to return the trunk as fast as possible, and both of us were thinking: Those journals were written in a state of great suffering and loneliness. Who knows what is secreted away in them?

I was visiting with Václav's wife and their children when he came downstairs again, after a surprisingly long time. Before he sat down, he laid a hand on my shoulder and said: "There's a footlocker, plus one more box filled with the same stuff as the trunk. He really wrote a lot."

That night I was having trouble sleeping when I heard someone walk quietly out of the master bedroom and downstairs. Right away I assumed it was Václav. When whoever it was didn't come back, I climbed out of bed and went downstairs too. It was him; he was sitting in an armchair, holding a book in one hand and smoking. We chatted amiably about our insomnia and what pills we took for it, then about our children and his wife. Neither one of us mentioned our burning the journals, but I'm sure he too could still see the flames as Dad's dreams went up in smoke—and the big bed where Dad had spent most of his last decade, tenaciously scribbling down all of his dreams, musings, and ideas; writing and writing because he had no one to tell them to. He had stopped yelling when we visited, and even smiled as he told us: "You barely know me, but thanks to these journals perhaps one day you will." We knew he was waiting for one of us to say, "So why don't you lend us a few right now?" But none of us ever did.

So this wooden footlocker was the one he took with him when he set off as a first-year recruit at the turn of the century. Here are all of his journals, neatly stacked in chronological order, with a handwritten label on the lid that says DREAMS.

"How come it's pink inside?"

"Not what you would expect, is it?"

"But why pink? Were all of his dreams pretty?"

"I think a lot of them were, or at least he would have used that word to describe them. At any rate I'm sure his dreams seemed better than real life in the twenty years after his suicide. I deliberately don't say 'suicide attempt,' because he actually went through with it. The fact that it failed—that stupid word again!—was not up to him; that was God's doing, as his friend Příbáň kept telling him: 'Stop your whining already, and just submit!'"

Dream journal no. 57, 1946

I stood on the terrace, sadly gazing into the garden. It was gloomy beneath the tall, leafy trees. Not a single ray of sunlight penetrated to the earth, all I could see was a glimmer here and there in the distance. Then suddenly I held my breath as the glimmer took the shape of a woman whom I instantly recognized as Eliška walking silently through the trees. I watched and waited. At last she came over, even smiling at me. She looked as she had in her youth: slender, almost ethereal, in a white dress, her long hair flowing down freely. She climbed the stairs and stopped at the last one, her left foot perched on the edge of the terrace, so that the shape of her long, slim leg was clearly visible beneath her straight skirt. A sheer white scarf, nearly reaching the ground, slipped from her right shoulder to her right hand as it rested on the stone balustrade. She stood peacefully, her gray-green eyes, like the water nymph Rusalka's, shining with confidence and contentment; her face, when she raised it to me, was cheerful. We had a brief conversation, quite pleasant and relaxed. I don't know what it was about, unfortunately, I can't even remember hearing her voice. As we spoke, she stepped onto the terrace and walked steadily toward the door to the bedroom. I made as if to escort her and noticed no resistance on her part. Although the ivy-framed doorway seemed very narrow, when I sized it up in my mind I could tell that it was wide enough for two if we walked closely side by side with our arms about each other's waist. Before we could reach the door, however, I awoke.

I am peaceful.

So, what do you think?" Libuše asked.

"Well, you know. We could talk on and on about the meaning of each and every word. It's all bubbling up inside me. The terrace, the garden, the leafy trees—of course that's Grandpa's old house, Dad always loved that place. Mom as a young woman. Just the two of them, still carefree, enjoying a nice, relaxed conversation. But even so, his sadness and gloom still managed to work their way in. He never did like dusk. Dreary days frightened him. They made him sad even when nothing else was wrong."

"And then he quickly made sure that something was."

"He must have been quite sensitive to air pressure."

"And colors. I've noticed that in every one of these dreams Mom is wearing a white dress."

"He loved white."

"Red too, though. He liked everything red. Red is cheerful, and cheerfulness was the one thing he could never attain. When he said someone was cheerful, that was the highest recommendation he could give. He loved cheerful music, he refused to read sad books, and the only paintings he wanted around were cheerful ones."

"That really aggravated me. It was as though his lordship were denying any other art the right to exist."

"I think all of us were annoyed by his insistence on cheerfulness. I can still see him now, walking up to the table—the soup has already been served—eagerly rubbing his hands, he gives us all a happy look, and says: 'All right, now we're going to be cheerful.' And as soon as he said it, we all turned into zombies."

"Absolutely. Sorry, though. I'm still thinking about those colors. They both liked red, actually. Both of them liked that red armchair in the sunroom, and Mom used to dress us in red all the time—and whenever we showed Dad a new outfit that was red, he would go out of his way to compliment us. Mom had the same hair color and complexion as us, but she never wore red—because she was sad inside, I suppose. And as for Dad, seeing Eliška in red probably would have been too much for him; he always liked her better in white. White was cheerful too, but in a delicate, moderate way."

"Right, and he must have known that glimmer in the dark was Mom—even before he recognized her. Why else would he have held his breath?"

"Well, that's the key to it all. The light was Eliška. In 1946, when he had that dream, he was seventy-one, they had been divorced twelve years, and still Eliška was his shining light. Yet even in his dream he doesn't race over to her, call out, or wave; instead he just stands there worrying that she won't come, and then at last when she does, she even gives him a smile."

"The first time Mom and Dad saw each other after the divorce was by accident, while I was in the sanatorium after having my first child. Both of them were stunned. When Dad walked in, Mom just stared straight ahead, frozen stiff. He bowed politely, said hello, and walked past her to my bed. For a little while we talked, and then, without another word, he stiffly walked back out again. As soon as the door had shut, I burst out laughing: 'Lord, what do you two think you're doing? And Mom, you're the one who started it! That's not like you, what was that supposed to mean?' She was as flustered as a little girl. She blanched, blushed, and then apologized profusely. She said she didn't know what came over her, but she was so afraid of insulting him that she couldn't make up her mind whether to stay or go."

"Maybe she was worried that your milk would dry up, and that's why she didn't want to tell you she was scared of him, and still somewhat disgusted—that's an awful word, isn't it? Do you remember at the end of the war one day over breakfast that time she told us one of her dreams? Maybe you had already left home by then. And by the way, it's fascinating how all it takes is a year or two in age difference, even with all that brothers and sisters have in common, and it's as though we were all living in different worlds. There are so many events we miss—we don't notice, or nobody tells us because we're too little, or maybe we're sick, or away from home. All it takes is one little thing for a major family event to pass us by, or vice versa, to affect us deeply."

But to return to Mom's dream: She dreamed that she was still married, and she was terrified. She kept telling herself: No, it can't be, what's happening? Everything was fine, I was free again—or could it have been just a dream? And then she woke up bathed in sweat and was overjoyed to find that, yes, it really had been a dream, and in real life she was still free.

"And maybe that same night Dad dreamed that she was the light in the darkness. He was always so shy, except when he got angry—even in the dream he waited to see what she would do when she saw him—and when she even smiled at him, he was in bliss."

Even as Libuše and I planned our reconnaissance of the attic, we knew it was going to be more depressing than exhilarating, so we agreed that we should do it together and promised ourselves not to get too emotional. For a boost, we brought along a big pot of tea, strawberry wafers, and a box of chocolate-coated cherries. After nibbling away in silence for a while, Libuše, her mouth still full, said:

"I keep thinking about those words *almost ethereal,* and the nymph. What do you make of it?"

"Boy oh boy, let me tell you! One day, in front of our aunts and uncles, Dad said, 'How about that Eliška! Still a little girl, still a nymph—and come to think of it, a true Czech athlete, too!' A general embarrassment resulted, as if he had said something he wasn't supposed to, as if somewhere between the nymph and the athlete a painful secret lay hidden."

"That ethereal gentleness, attractive and elusive, that was the nymph, right?"

"And the strength was the athlete."

"Do you realize that Mom and Dad never sang together? Yet they both loved to sing and had beautiful voices. Whenever Aunt Klára came to visit, Dad would beg her to sing the Moon in the Heavens aria from Dvořák's *Rusalka,* and then he would embarrass us by crooning, 'Oh where can you be, O sweet nymph of mine.'"

"I know about that white dress and the free-flowing hair."

In a rare moment of good humor, with his first grandson seated on his lap, suddenly Dad said one day: "It isn't true that life has brought me nothing but bad and that all I do is complain. There have been good things too, and I'm grateful for them." Then he told me the story of one of his reunions with Mom when he was on leave from the army: "I rode the train all night and didn't arrive until early the next morning. I walked in the door and caught your mother in her robe in front of the mirror before she had tied up her hair. You may not recall, but when she sat down, her hair reached almost all the way to the ground! She had the most magnificent long brown hair!" Then for a long time he just sat there. The child didn't make any fuss, and I didn't breathe a word. Both Dad and I were remembering the old master bedroom—where all four of us had been born—with the dressing table between the windows that let in the morning sun. Mom sat there brushing her hair, the bed no doubt still rumpled, with the intoxicating fragrance of home all around.

"Let me go on: 'She stood peacefully, her gray-green eyes, like the water nymph Rusalka's, shining with confidence and contentment; her face, when she raised it to me, was cheerful.' Now do you see why he painted his footlocker pink inside? And why he said: 'Now the gods are on my side. Otherwise they wouldn't send me such beautiful dreams'?"

"It's fascinating the way everything he longed for comes together. Here he is, living in a constant state of agitation, stress, and doubt, and suddenly, of her own accord, she comes and stands calmly before him. In other words, there's no danger of her leaving soon; on the contrary, it raises his hopes for more. Her eyes shine with confidence and contentment, so he doesn't have to worry that the glow will suddenly be extinguished, confirming not only that she's peaceful but that she's content and—best of all—cheerful!"

Our parents' sad yearning for cheerfulness.

One day Mom bought a Gothic Madonna with a large teardrop running down her cheek. Dad was outraged at the idea of such a sad thing in the house, so she put it in the sunroom, next to her piano. Then one day, as she walked into the dining room, Dad asked: "How can you do that? For a whole hour you play nothing but sad music and look at that sad thing, and then you come out of there beaming?"

"They do my crying for me," she replied.

I was still in kneesocks at the time. On hearing her first sentence, I decided to make myself scarce, and in my hurry to get upstairs I stumbled on the first step and scraped off a scab on my knee. I can remember sitting on the ground lamenting the fact that I had to fall on my bad knee; probably that was what gave her words time to sink in.

"We still haven't talked about their 'sex tragedy' either, as Aunt Blažena referred to it."

"Aunt Blažena told me that someone had to sleep with Mom after every birth or miscarriage so that Dad wouldn't harass her. She or Grandma would come in and pretend to be helping the nurse."

"I heard that from her too. Grandma was smarter; she

kept quiet about it. I was sixteen when I found out, and afterward I couldn't even look at him. Then when I did have to deal with him, no doubt I was sharp as a razor. How do you feel about it now?"

"You mean you see it differently now? I would just as soon not even think about it."

"Come on, Dad was no rapist. Passionate, headstrong, impulsive, unruly, yes, all of those things, but—I just thought of something. Do you remember how much Mom liked *The Riddle of Helen* by Houghton? President Masaryk was quoted in the newspaper as saying it was one of the most intriguing books he had ever read, and Mom cut out the article. If I remember correctly, Helen did herself in (again, a terrible phrase, I realize, but 'committing suicide' isn't any better) because both of the men she loved were madly in love with her womanhood (that was what the article said) yet they failed to see her as a human being."

"All right, all right, I can see what you mean, and actually I've been thinking the same thing for ages. Mom longed for a partnership of equals, and all Dad wanted was a fragile little pussycat whose every flaw he would happily forgive as long as she cried a lot and snuggled up to him after every 'sin.' She could lie, cheat, and deceive, but she had to be the ivy wound around his trunk—those were the very words of Aunt Blažena, the model wife."

"As Mom added: 'wound so tight it chokes the tree to death.'"

"It wouldn't have even mattered except that he didn't realize it until—like Uncle Tomáš—it was too late. Just so long as he was the master and commander in chief, whose wife looked up to him with undying admiration and doglike devotion. Just like Aunt Blažena, or the fictional Mrs. Kondelíková, who always made a point of feeding her husband his favorite soup before she spoke her mind."

"Now hold on! That's both true and it isn't. Maybe Dad

would have been happy with a pussycat like Mrs. Kondelíková, and odds are they would have led a more or less comfortable life, or at least had a normal, quarrelsome marriage.
But that doesn't change the fact that he loved Mom body
and soul all his life."

"Oh God! Why is it that some of us are the embodiment
of every desire for so many people of different dispositions,
and on several different levels, while others have to search
and search before they find the one who's right? Only the
Cosmic Director knows."

"We could go on like this until our heads are spinning.
But have we said anything new? What have we figured out?"

"That at first it was their differing dispositions. By that I
don't mean Dad's depressions and anxiety, which he so often
covered up with rage, or Mom's love of life and optimism,
which she constantly cloaked in sadness, although someday
we can come back to both of those. What I'm talking about
is the fact that Dad was a product of the nineteenth century—in upbringing and disposition. After all, in 1900 he was
twenty-seven years old! While Mom, on the other hand,
could easily have been a woman of the late twentieth century. I don't think I need to spell it out. That was the reason
why he hurt her and couldn't understand her, or she him,
and that's also why she didn't realize it. She just fought tooth
and nail to keep from being like Aunt Blažena or Mrs.
Kondelíková. As far as Dad was concerned, they were mas-
ters of feminine diplomacy, and he meant it with respect; but
for Mom they were pitiful. . . . Why don't you stop me
already, before I drown in this stuff!"

"Don't worry, there are two of us here. But let's go back
to what happened while she was recovering from giving
birth."

"All right. Well, today I can't imagine Dad ever forcing
Mom to fulfill her marital duties. After all, we know how
shy he always was. Just look, even in his dream he didn't

budge until she had walked past him without stopping—he didn't dare. But then he had to, or she would have walked away. All that talk about sizing up the door was only a pretense so he could think about holding her—and then the mere thought of it made him so giddy that he immediately dropped it in favor of just an arm around her shoulders or waist. And even that upset him so much he woke up.

"In short, today I see his need to express his urges in a different light. I understand Mom's reaction, floating as she was in the rapture of motherhood: 'All he ever thinks about is doing it.' But there was no need for him to be insulted and humiliated; the truth is, calling in her mother and sister as guards was an awful thing to do. Dad wasn't some wild animal, but a man who loved and desired his wife. They could have avoided all the aggravation and provocation, the flare-ups over and over, with him screaming and yelling and hideous. . . . So say something already."

"Oh, all right. First, I just remembered that it was the idea of that experienced old doctor; he told Grandma about it and recommended protection. And if even *he* couldn't think of anything smarter, what were they supposed to do? Second, as for taking an impartial view of the way things were between them, we don't know enough to do that. But more important, we've got other nuts to crack. Our share in it is primarily about *us*. So why don't we leave it at that for today?"

"Fine. But if you could just hold on for those last three words of his: 'I am peaceful.' What do you make of that?"

"Well, maybe it means that when he woke up, he didn't fly out of bed as if he'd been bitten, or break a window or anything, but just silently rode out the storm of emotions unleashed by the dream. Remember how he used to say: 'Last night I woke up sweating like a pig four times, and I didn't have anything to change into'? Well, that was the way things were—we just chalked it up to nerves, what did we know? Only this time, overcome with pain, he lay there calmly, stretched out long and thin. When the pins and needles in his legs escalated into violent spasms, he weighted them down with a couple volumes of *Otto's Encyclopedia* on top of the covers and calmly smoked a few cigarettes, the glowing tip in his trembling old hand bobbing in the darkness. Then he switched on the light, put on his glasses, and wrote the dream down in his journal. After all, he had to tell someone."

And then one day there was an unusually long line in the dairy market under the arcade, and a little ways in front of me I glimpsed an old man's fingers wrapped around a crutch handle and wearing a familiar old-fashioned ring. I couldn't believe it. I took a small step out of line, as if trying to see what they had on the counter—and indeed it was him, my elderly gentleman. But he no longer towered over everyone. I might have stood on line with him a dozen times and not noticed that he was there too: stooped over and no longer tall, propped up on two crutches.

I felt so sorry for him!

His dapper, frayed elegance was gone. Everything about him was shabby and run-down. A misshapen old briefcase hung from a worn leather strap around his neck, leaving his hands free to grip the crutches. Suddenly I remembered the dog and glanced out through the glass doors. Seeing no sign of him, I left my place in line to go have a look outside. He wasn't there. On top of everything else, even his dog was gone! My mind was made up.

The next day was a gorgeous May Saturday. On a day like this, Dad would have taken a tram to the end of the line, out of Prague, into the sunshine. And on a day like this, the elderly gentleman might be in the park on Kampa. My guess was correct; there he was, sitting on a bench.

I sat down next to him: "May I?" He politely doffed his hat and replied, "Of course." I waited a while and then inquired about his dog.

He turned to me—"How kind of you to ask"—and again doffed his hat. "I am so terribly old," he said, letting the emphasis on *old* sink in, "and it is so very nice, truly, to be addressed by a lady such as yourself."

We sat for a while in silence.

"Yes, old Roland is dead. It will be six months now."

"His name was Roland?"

"Roland, yes. He was given that name ages ago!"

Surely, I thought, he must have memories dating back further than the life span of a dog. Perhaps he only meant that a great deal had happened in the course of Roland's life. I also got the feeling that it wasn't he who had named the dog, but I didn't dare ask. Instead I told him the story of how I had come to meet Roland, and how after that he always remembered me and greeted me with affection. The elderly gentleman smiled as I spoke, nodding his head and gazing off into the distance.

"So," he said, "the scoundrel (Dad's word!) kept secrets from me, did he?" Then he went on smiling and gazing into the distance.

I didn't dare say anything more, none of that "You must be sad now that he's gone. When such a faithful companion dies, it's like losing a close friend." No, nothing of the sort. It didn't feel right.

Our conversation moved on to the weather, then to the dandelions beaming yellowly on the lawn in front of us, then to the children darting back and forth, and again we praised the gorgeous weather. It was all rather casual and impersonal, but then I started to talk about how my slipped disc acts up when the weather is bad. When he didn't join in as expected, I moved on to the medical center and the produce shop and all of the rest, and suddenly he realized that I had been observing him for years. He turned and fixed me with a long, hard look, but I held his gaze right back. Go ahead and look, I thought, I've got nothing to hide.

Finally the elderly gentleman settled back, lowering his

head as if to indicate the topic was closed, and said: "The pipits came so early this year, I was starting to worry they had made a mistake."

It was as if he had given me the opening note for us to launch into the symphony.

"My dad," I said, picking up on the pipits, "also paid a lot of attention to birds. He would take note of what time each one started to sing and tell us about it over breakfast. Some birds start while it's still dark, he said, but they only chirp; their songs don't really begin until daybreak. He said that each species had a starting time so precise it would put the railroads to shame. Not only did we not believe him; we didn't even listen to what he said. To us it was just boring. Years later, though, I read an ornithology article confirming what he had told us—perhaps there were a few seasonal differences, I don't recall—and that started me thinking about my dad's insomnia, because that was the basis of his bird watching."

Once again the elderly gentleman turned to face me. After studying me for a moment, he lowered his eyes and settled back. His neck was stiff, and even turning his head a little gave him difficulties.

A little boy with a scooter came running up to us to show off his bell. As we took turns ringing it, I continued: "Then one day my dad came down to breakfast and started talking about the birds as if they were second-graders: 'All of the birds are on time,' he said. 'Only the cuckoo is always tardy.' We started laughing so hard we barely noticed him glance around in bewilderment and then leave the room without eating. All day long after that, as we played inside the house and out in the garden, we shouted back and forth to one another, 'The cuckoo is always tardy!'"

I didn't realize I was still ringing the bell until the elderly gentleman took my hand, gave it a gentle squeeze, and laid it back in my lap.

A few days later, I noticed him looking around as I

walked toward the bench. He spotted me and raised his hat in greeting. I didn't know it at the time, but later on he told me that he had been looking forward to our next encounter as much as I had.

The moment I took my seat beside him, however, we were both overcome with bashfulness. It took a while for the words to emerge from inside us again. Apologizing for not having introduced himself sooner, the elderly gentleman ceremoniously offered me his calling card—prewar, judging from the style and typeface: *Doctor of Jurisprudence Radim Bukovanský.* It gave two addresses, one in Prague, the other in southern Bohemia. I too introduced myself, adding a few more bits of information, but he declined to reveal any more about himself. It soon became clear that we were both allowing time for the peculiar process that was happening inside us to run its course. I believe we both felt it, without any need to understand or resist.

A dozen times I had some memory of Dad on the tip of my tongue, and a dozen times I left it unspoken to surface in its own time. I chose not to entrust anything to words, but as the story unfolded within me, in the elderly gentleman's peculiar proximity, I saw it projected before him with a fresh, impersonal, brilliant clarity.

Everyone called him Old Valenta, even though he probably wasn't all that old. He had a young wife and two little children, but he himself was somewhat shabby-looking. I don't know why. We preferred not to think about it since our dad always forced it on us.

On payday, which was Saturday, Old Valenta would go out and drink so much beer that he couldn't get home on his own. He must have realized the state he was in, however, because instead of walking home from the pub the way he came—through town, where everyone could see him—he would take the path called simply "between the fences," which ran behind the pub. On one side of the path was our garden wall; on the other, a thick, prickly hedge of hawthorn marking the boundary of the Stloukalů family orchard. Old Valenta tried his best to keep to the side without prickers, but there was nothing for him to hold onto, so he would end up staggering into the hedge, and then he was too loaded to get himself out. Once we had gotten over our fright at the sound of his moaning, groaning, and wailing, we would scramble up the bushes, into the trees, and onto the wall so we could see what was going on, and then go and fetch the gardener to help him. The gardener, when he could be persuaded, would come and douse Old Valenta with a bucket full of water, drag him out of the hedge, stand him up, and escort him the rest of the way down the treacherous path. More often than not, however, the gardener said that he was too busy. So sometimes Granny Nečasová would help out Old Valenta. As he lay dozing, she would give him a piece of her mind, and only after that would she shake him awake and help him to his feet. Then all the way back to his house she would carp: "Tell me how do I always git wrapped up in this? That's the last time you catch *me* between them stupid fences!" Most passersby, though, when they saw the stinking drunk just spat in the dirt and hurried along their way.

On Saturdays, Dad would come to take afternoon tea in the garden. We couldn't hear a thing from where we sat, but when the maid came to clear the table, she reported that Old Valenta was laid out in the thorns again. The first time Dad found himself in the area at the crucial moment, it was by chance, while he was out on a stroll before supper. But from then on, he would return to that spot again and again, absolutely intentionally, at the same time every Saturday. He even put a crate in the bushes so he could climb on top and see over the wall to the path. Then he would lie in wait for the moment when Old Valenta's children appeared. The worst was listening to the little boy's muffled voice, patient and good-natured, as he reasoned with his father: "Cripes, Paw, why ya gotta make it so dang hard on us? Just try and move a little so's we can lift ya." Then the little girl would chime in: "Aw, come on, Paw!" It broke our dad's heart. He would anxiously dart back and forth, one minute nestling up to the wall like a baby to its mother's breast, the next hammering it with his fists like a madman.

Those children didn't have it easy. On their own, they were able to drag their father out of the hedge and pluck out the thorns—"Gee, look at the blood!"—but to get him on his feet they had to have help, either from Old Valenta himself, depending on how drunk he was and how long he had been passed out, or from a chance passerby. Otherwise, they would give up talking and squat down next to their father for a while, watching his beard rise and fall with his snores, and then walk off without a word. That half-hour it took before the children returned must have been excruciating for Dad. When at last they reappeared with a wheelbarrow, they would load up their father, audibly panting, puffing, and cursing with the effort. Finally they would tie him in with rope so he wouldn't fall out, and trundle him off. "All righty, now home you go," the little girl said, and our dad, listening behind the wall, softly added: "Amen."

Whether anyone besides me ever spied on Dad I don't know. I hope not. But I never told anyone about it. After the episodes with Old Valenta, Dad would always arrive at the dinner table in a strangely ambivalent mood: on the one hand, exhilarated; yet on the other, ominously maudlin, almost meek. Noticing how quiet he was, we lifted our heads from our plates and were startled by his eyes, so incongruous for a man of his age — the eyes of a little boy peering out at the world from his stroller, or of the deer we used to surprise in the park.

Even worse was when he would launch into his tirade: "So what would you do if I were like Old Valenta? Would you take care of me the way his children do, or would you be ashamed? If you saw me lying by the side of the road, would you admit that I was your father, or would you be embarrassed and run away? Well, come on then, what would you do? You would run off and leave your daddy lying in the mud, wouldn't you? Just tell the truth!"

He was only kidding to start with, but then he kept pushing and prodding us, until finally he was screaming: "You would sooner have me croak like some mangy old dog than admit to anyone that that drunk lying in the mud stinking of piss was your father. Come on now, I want an answer!"

First we tried logic: "If Mr. Valenta were our father and Mrs. Valenta were our mother, then we would be their children. . . ." But no, he wouldn't hear of it. Dad wanted all of us, his children and his wife, to prove our love for him by accepting him as is, as automatically as the Valenta children accepted their own father: always and everywhere, no matter what. If they could do it, why couldn't we?

"Because . . . because," we began, but then all we could

do was sit there, speechless and embarrassed, until finally we burst into tears. It did no good for Mom to explain that children like us, who had been raised differently and who were accustomed to seeing their father in control of himself—

"Precisely! That's precisely it!" our father broke in. "If it were to happen one day—and it could, you know, it can happen even to the most upstanding individual—then that is all the more reason why they ought to take care of their father!"

"But that isn't the case with Old Valenta," Mom said. "Please just don't try to make them imagine what it's like to be both your children and his."

No, he refused. He could see himself clearly: clothes in tatters, dead drunk, snoring away in the gutter, and us on the sidewalk, gaping at him with fear and revulsion until at last, flustered, we give up and flee. He claimed to know "without any doubt whatsoever"—he not only knew, he *felt*, and here he quoted Corinthians: "knowledge puffeth up, but charity edifieth"—that were it not for the fact that those children, *his* children, had that accursed foreign blood in them (now he was outright roaring), they wouldn't have run away.

Afterward the four of us were always afraid to look one another in the eye. We could all picture ourselves (at least I think so; we never spoke about it) standing on the sidewalk, just as he described, anxious and flustered, hoping our mom will appear. And when she doesn't turn up, we give up and flee, even though we know full well we should stay with our dad—my God, are we really as bad as he thinks?

The first two meetings were enough to make friends of us—almost relatives, in a strange way. True to my nature, I was the more talkative one, while the elderly gentleman remained in his shell. Perhaps he had been born that way, or perhaps he had simply been holed up in there for so long that to him it felt natural.

I made time for the elderly gentleman at least once a

week. On my way home from the university library I would take the Charles Bridge, and if the weather was nice I would stop off in the park on Kampa or the Vojan Gardens, depending on what we had agreed; if the weather was bad, I went to his place. Unfortunately the elderly gentleman was unable to visit me because my building had no elevator and I lived too high up for him to walk. Often I brought with me something I had prepared at home beforehand—not always, though, since he enjoyed playing host. Otherwise I did the cooking while we sat and talked in his kitchen. We both liked that best, I think. Naturally it made me remember that I never cooked for my dad; I never stayed long enough. Instead I always brought something ready-made and only sat down for a few minutes while Dad scurried about like a conscientious housewife, offering me one thing after another: fruit, chocolate, candy, crackers, cigarettes, whatever he could think of to entice me to stay a little longer. I was always in a hurry, though, and preferred to have him over to our place. I felt safer at home. And besides, the children and visitors coming and going served as a good distraction.

But to return to the elderly gentleman.

We were both aware of what a remarkable friendship we had, and accepted every one of our shared opinions and understandings as if it were heaven-sent. At one point we both confessed that we had never felt so reluctant to be so close to someone, and yet so open, so free. What enabled us to meet—or as we put it, to find each other—was the vigilance with which we responded to our inner guidance, even on those occasions when it caused tension.

This trust and reliance on instinct had a larger impact than we realized at the time. Undoubtedly it was one of the things that made our connection so special, so unique, although it would be wrong to imply that it was anything like a father-daughter relationship, especially not in the typical sense.

In fact it resembled more the relationship that began

when the forty-year-old Karla Jasanová (Caroline Jason), living in Chicago, received a letter addressed to her deceased mother from the Czechoslovak embassy. In it, Karla learned that she was not alone in the world but had a father living in Prague.

Acting on impulse, Karla immediately disposed of all her belongings and moved to Prague. As it turned out, after years of mourning the wife who had abandoned him, her father had remarried. More important, however, as Karla and her father came to know each other, slowly, step by step, they came to discover that they were two of a kind and got along famously.

This was the true story of my first English teacher, and I myself took comfort in their happy ending more than once. I could see how careful Karla and her father were not to interfere in or disrupt each other's life in any way, although it goes without saying that they each had their own habits. Among Karla's many idiosyncrasies, she had a different way of cooking, a different way of housekeeping, a different taste in clothes—after all, she was still Miss Caroline Jason. But whenever I saw them together at concerts, they sat closely side by side, and walked out at intermission holding hands. It must have been the music that put them so at ease, because whenever she went to his house or he visited her apartment, they were incredibly formal with each other. Mr. Jasan would never say "Hi" or even "Hello," but always "What a pleasure to see you," kissing her on the cheek only after he had kissed her hand. Still, Karla enjoyed it, and although she always paused for a second to consider asking him to stop, in the end she kept her mouth shut and gave her father a big hug, and then the two of them would laugh together. It always took a while before they felt comfortable enough first to pour the tea and then to add the sugar. They never truly relaxed until the conversation turned to books, and then they would talk until their ears burned. They were even able to argue and get angry at each other. But invariably their disputes would conclude in laughter and long loving looks.

In her free time, Karla liked to paint. But while her father favored modern art, Karla loved the nineteenth-century realists, preferring to do loose adaptations of Jaroslav Čermák. Still, even that worked out. Her father would sit in an armchair next to the easel, taking pleasure in watching his daughter paint as he smoked his pipe and chatted with her.

How could I fail to think of those two when I "started in" with Eldergent? Many times I told myself that they had provided me with excellent training, though of course our relationship had more levels to it than the Jasans'. Nevertheless, for whatever reason, it never occurred to either of us to treat each other as father and daughter; it even seemed sometimes that we were both at pains to avoid that type of relationship at all costs. Our respect for each other had increased to the point that either of us would have considered it a threat to the other's independence. And yet, every so often something so extraordinarily nice would happen between us that we wanted to give it a name—it was like a small, warm spring quietly bubbling up to the surface. Eventually we decided that we must have been father and daughter in a previous life, and that reassured us.

It took nearly two years for us to tell each other all that, but when it came to other topics we moved more quickly. Things would suddenly come up the way they had when I blurted out the business about Dad and the cuckoo on our second encounter, and it never occurred to us that it might be strange. Oddly enough, it didn't matter that I talked all about myself while he rarely spoke about or exposed anything of himself. What mattered was that he accepted my need to confess, yet rather than playing the silent willow he was an involved, active listener, and always urged me on—"I beg you, please continue"—as if every word I said were of particular relevance for him.

As he himself put it so pithily, his childhood had been wonderful, his younger years good; he had had trouble finding the right woman, and married late. Once he found her, they lived happily together until the war, when he was sent to Dachau. He was there almost five years. When the Communists came to power in Czechoslovakia in 1948, his wife wanted them to leave the country, but he persuaded her to take their daughter and go without him.

"I wanted to find out what would happen, I wanted to be part of it. After all, not everyone could leave, right?"

Three years later, his wife asked for a divorce and took a new husband.

"That I could understand, even if it was painful—only why hasn't she written? And my daughter's silence is still harder to take. I believed there was love between us. She was sixteen years old when they left. Three years ago she began sending me a few postcards and letters each year. But in every line I read, I can sense that she doesn't know what to say."

"Is that so surprising? Do you try to make it any easier for her?"

But I don't want to get into that now. I'm not here to tell stories, but to unload my burden and settle my debts.

Have you ever been suddenly wrenched out of sleep in the middle of the night, when you sit bolt upright, staring into the dark, eyes wide open, and suddenly something that has been clouded and confused for years becomes clear to you?

The facts were not in my dad's favor. After twenty-six years of marriage, he asked his wife for a divorce on the night before she left for the sanatorium with a serious illness; he fell for a girl more than thirty years his junior; and then, after fouling everything up and leading the family business to the brink of bankruptcy, he committed a suicide that failed.

It has been more than forty years, but I can still remember the feeling of helpless confusion that washed over us at first. (My memory is like a double exposure: I can picture the four of us, almost fully grown up, by the side of his bed, and the six-month-old Kristýnka, with a painful ear infection, pawing at her head and bawling as she anxiously scans the room.) Next, moving through the spectrum of reactions, came shame and embarrassment, followed by outrage and condemnation, and then, at the very end, a cluster of pity and compassion for the poor unfortunate who was in so much pain, even if through his own doing.

By then I believe we had perfected our technique of "not thinking about it," with *it* representing all the suffering in our family with which we were unable to come to terms. We didn't think about what it had been like for him to reach that decision, what it had been like buying a ticket to the mountains — "First class, sir?" — so as not to sully the family home, getting off at the little station and walking up into the woods where he had taught his children to ski. I can still remember how by the time we had hiked all the way up to the cottage, our four little knapsacks would all be hanging off the outside of his massive pack. And how once I needed to pee during the long walk up and wet my pants right there, in the middle of a blizzard, and Dad took out his big handkerchief, all toasty warm from his body, and tucked it inside my pants. . . .

Unless you spontaneously fall into each other's arms, I can hardly imagine anything more awkward than a visit to someone after a failed suicide. What do you say? Everything seems inappropriate, pointless, irrelevant. The four of us stood around our dad's bed a while before citing his frail condition as an excuse to leave a short time later. Libuše was the only one who stayed with him. Some time later, I asked her what it had been like, and her reply was curt: "Same as ever. It broke my heart, but I didn't know how to act natural and show him what I was feeling. He even asked why I had stayed behind instead of leaving with the rest of you, but of course I couldn't explain, so I just sat there without saying anything."

It was much the same for me when I took Libuše's place a week later. I did my best to make him comfortable—bringing him his favorite blanket and pillow, making him meals that I knew he couldn't taste—and yet, at the same time I despised myself for being so unnatural and mechanical about it. I could picture myself as a girl in a movie, one of those grim sergeant types who walks around as if she has swallowed a ruler, grinding her teeth. No matter how hard I fought the stony feeling, it shot through my body, leaving me in a constant state of pain and stress.

The worst was when Mom came to visit, calm and concerned, as though one of us had come down with a fever and no one knew what the matter was yet.

Upon arriving, she asked me not to tell Dad that she was there until I thought the time was right.

But when I tried, Dad just shook his head furiously: "No, no, no! So that's why it suddenly got so hard to breathe in here—it's because *she* is near." Then his voice gave out, but his lips went on forming the words that I now knew practically by heart.

I relayed the message to Mom, and she simply nodded her head: "I'll go for a walk around town and maybe he'll be in a better mood by the time I get back."

I didn't say a word, but inside me a storm was raging. My mom had put the past behind her and come all this way. Now here she was, wandering an unfamiliar city, dazed from lack of sleep and still weak from her own recent stay in the sanatorium, yet she was worried to death about the rest of us, including Dad. Could it be that she still cared for him, even if only in a motherly way?

My dad and I passed an hour or so in silence, and then he asked gruffly: "Where is she?"

"She went out for a walk, but she'll be back in case you change your mind."

Stammering but exultant, he replied: "Get out there and wait, and when she comes, you can tell her to turn right back around and leave, and that's an order!"

I got up and started out the door, but then, thinking I would save Mom the trouble of sending me back in, I turned and asked: "So is that your final decision?"

My tone of voice was neither placating nor conciliatory. It was dripping with anger, although I probably halfway hoped that it really was the last word on the matter. Dad nodded sullenly.

But the day wasn't over yet. Not half an hour after my mother had left, Dad asked once again, even more rudely than before, if possible: "Where is she?"

"You wanted her gone, so she left."

"That she-devil! To think such a lofty woman would visit such a wretch!" I was shaking so hard my teeth chattered, but I managed to keep my mouth shut as he went on: "On her knees she should have come crawling! On her knees!"

He continued in that horrible vein for a while before pausing to catch his breath for the next outburst (all that talking tired him out, and it also must have been painful, because the bullet had passed through just a millimeter above his heart). Wearying of his diatribe, I finally decided to speak:

"When are you going to realize that it's no one's fault but your own that your idea of reality is so far from the truth? Why should Mom, of all people, come crawling to you?!" With that I walked out and didn't return again until the next day.

He slept that night—they gave him shots and pills—and as for me, the only thing that kept me from doing myself in was my love for Mom. I couldn't stand the grief—the grief and the helplessness. What was I supposed to do? What could I do when he was so vicious to Mom and yet in so much pain himself?

The next morning I found Dad lying quietly in bed, eyes closed. He heard me enter the room and slowly lifted his eyelids to watch me take off my coat and sit down on the chair next to his bed. Then his eyes closed again, and though they stayed that way all day long, I could tell from his face that he was silently slipping deeper and deeper into despair.

A few days later (or was it months?), the doctor told him that he was recovered. Dad opened his eyes wide in terror and his entire body stiffened. His face muscles went into spasms as he gritted his teeth, pitching his head frantically from side to side. No, no, no! He didn't want to hear it! He didn't want to be better. Before he could speak, however, the doctor signaled the nurse to give him a shot. Dad understood the signal and toppled over in bed like a tree. He closed his eyes and surrendered to desperation, plunging deeper and deeper into its agonizing caves and caverns. At last I couldn't stand it anymore: I took his hand and fell with him.

To tell the truth, though, not for long. Dad moved from the hospital straight to Prague, where his brother, Uncle Vincent, had found an apartment for him. None of us came to help him settle in. Apart from the "spell" we were under and our self-centeredness, I think it was mainly youth's natural instinct for self-preservation. Our old cook was the only one who went to stay with him, since, as our mom put it, "What would the master do on his own?"

So began Dad's twenty years of not-life, not-death.

I don't like saying so, even today it's not easy, but the truth is that we accepted the whole thing as the final solution to all of our family problems—Dad's request for a divorce, his affair with the girl, even the disaster that resulted in his moving to Prague—it suited us.

My brothers adopted the pose of knights championing their jilted mother's honor, and didn't turn up at his doorstep even once during the first few years that he was in Prague. They only began to soften during the war, and even then it was slow going. Only Libuše and I, as the caring females, occasionally paid him a visit. The first Christmas I went to stay with Dad with the feeling I was deserting my family, and it was so stressful—annoyed at what he assumed was an act of mercy, he forced me to listen to him rail against my mother every day—that my sister and I agreed never to make that mistake again. Even after Libuše got married and moved to Prague and started seeing him more regularly, for Christmas she would always go home, meaning to Mom's.

Maybe we really were all caught in a spell, although Mom less so than the rest of us. Maybe that was what made us forget him, even glad to be rid of him, and not think about how he was doing.

He was right to say that we didn't understand him. But by the same token, probably none of us was mistaken to think: At least I understand you a little, whereas you don't understand me one bit!

Still, we admitted that when it came to certain things, we didn't know beans. For instance, we always liked to say that Dad was a nuisance to everyone, including himself. But whenever he was anywhere on his own—for instance, at the neurological sanatorium in Gräfenberk—he was always very well liked and highly respected by the other patients.

Every time one of us went to see him, we heard nothing but praise for our dad from all sides: what a thoughtful, attentive, marvelous companion, so sensitive and compassionate, listening to his fellow patients' most intimate thoughts for hours on end.

We always came back from those visits utterly flabbergasted. And we kept asking ourselves how it could be. For him to be putting on an act, as Uncle Ondřej suggested, was out of the question. We had never known him to do that, and given his precarious moods, we couldn't believe he was capable of acting for weeks at a time.

Everything about it was unbelievable, but particularly the idea of him as a compassionate listener. This was the man who let his children get out three sentences at best before interrupting with his annoying "Oh yes, I know, I remember when . . ." and launching into a half-hour monologue. But what galled us most was that he was never even aware he did it. Today I realize that his childhood memories were a cherished refuge for him, although according to Aunt Mára, not everything was as he portrayed it. Apparently he had often felt himself oppressed and persecuted, when the reality was they had all doted on him as the baby of the family.

Dad marvelous company? A sympathetic listener? It was a true mystery. It wasn't the only one, however, so we simply added it to all the others and didn't think any more of it.

Especially since the doctors painted quite a different picture, which corresponded to our own in every detail. With respectful amusement, they related the story of how Dad had nearly brought down the roof the first time they gave him a thermal wrap.

As the nurse finished bundling him into the wet sheet and woolen blanket, Dad had suddenly gotten it into his head that he wouldn't be able to free himself in time in the event a fire broke out. Flexing his arms and legs with all his might, he began to scream for help as if his life genuinely depended on it. For the next session the doctor made a point of coming in to show Dad how easy it was to loosen the covers, by rolling back and forth from one side to the other. That placated him, though he still insisted on testing it out a few times, with the nurse wrapping him up more loosely than usual, before he agreed to go ahead with the soothing treatment.

For us it was just another one of his embarrassing episodes. No one ever explained to us that Dad was genuinely sick—we ourselves had never heard of neurological disorders—and that therefore we shouldn't blame everything on his personality. (To what extent we exacerbated his condition by our own behavior of course now we will never know.)

If only that hideous crow would stop flapping around my head, croaking those words of Dad's over and over: "Why did you desert me? You could have talked me out of the divorce, but you were all so glad to be rid of me. It's one thing for a dad to ignore his kids, but when grown-up children do the same to their sixty-year-old father . . . ?"

To be sure, the divorce hadn't been our idea; it had never even crossed our minds that our parents might separate. As far as we were concerned, our suffering was just a cruel fact of life: It was our destiny. We preferred not to think about it. Once the possibility of divorce reared its head, however, we eagerly looked forward to the prospect of peace and quiet—and in a sense we got it.

That was why we didn't mind the affair with the young lady—the news spread at astonishing speed, probably because it was the last thing anyone expected from our father—and it was also why we so readily accepted the ridiculous version that filtered down to us. We preferred not to think about that either, when even the briefest reflection on Dad's timidness and modesty would have been enough to make us realize that he had never been the type to initiate a romantic liaison, and especially not given the terrible state he was in. (Without encouragement from his entire family, he never would have married at all, despite—or perhaps because of—the fact that he was so completely in love.)

Being as shy as he was, he started to coach us on assertiveness as soon as we were old enough to talk. On those rare occasions when he went with us for a Sunday stroll, he would always urge us to ask someone what time it was.

"But you've got a watch," we would say.

"Never mind that, just give it a try. It will be good for you. Don't be afraid," he would warmly encourage us.

We didn't understand, to us it just seemed silly and weird, but in the end we always humored him to keep from spoiling his good mood. With similar insistence, he would send us to the smoke shop to buy cigarettes and matches. One after the next, nice and orderly.

"There, you see? That didn't hurt too much now, did it?" he would greet us on our return.

"Why should it hurt?"

He was utterly baffled: "You mean you weren't shy?"

"When? Just now? No."

Sometimes it would sadden him: "Humph, must be that foreign blood." But most of the time he was genuinely pleased: "I'm glad to hear that, very glad indeed." Then he would confess to us how shy he was: at school, in church, in shops and restaurants. We pictured him as a shy little boy in a sailor's suit, and didn't realize until much later that he meant he was still that way.

He enjoyed strolling into a hotel restaurant, the well-bred gentleman out on the town with his lovely wife and four handsome children. No one would have suspected how tormented he was by the thought that he might fold under pressure. In front of his wife, the maître d', the doorman, everyone. To compensate for his lack of confidence, he would constantly clear his throat, and he was unnecessarily loud and hostile when placing his order. There we are, in the splendid hotel dining room, the waiters flitting noiselessly like blackbirds from one flowery table to the next, and our dad sits tensely, waiting for them to burst into laughter— "Ha ha ha! Ho ho ho!"—when he gets confused and chooses the wrong meal, and all the finely coiffed heads look up from their plates atop the sparkling silver tables, and a hush falls over the room, and everyone looks at us. They bow to his wife, give the children an approving nod, and he himself is condemned as hopeless.

Charles, our father's bachelor cousin (who had changed his name to Charles from Karel and fancied himself a bon vivant), was the one who introduced him to the young lady, claiming that it would help to distract him.

And Dad?

He had been stewing and smoldering inside for some time, as we now know, and his sixtieth birthday was the last straw, driving him into an alcoholiclike state of despair and desolation.

I didn't realize at the time that people's attitudes toward their birthdays have less to do with their views on formalities and decorum than with their frame of mind. It was only natural for Dad, feeling disoriented, dejected, and unloved, to want to be reassured that he wasn't really all that bad.

When that milestone rolled around, however, his children had been spending summers away from home for a good five years, by my reckoning, and their written congratulations (for the most part belated) were not exactly overflowing with love.

Both of our parents were determined to have us learn foreign languages, and so every summer they would send us away to study for two months—first German, then French, and then English. The first few summers Dad took the boys and Mom took the girls; later on, it was the brothers who escorted the sisters. I remember the first year we were in Austria: I was in a boarding school on Wörther See, in the south, and Libuše was on Attersee, to the north; they put us each in different places so we couldn't speak Czech together. The boys, too. The trip home was wonderful. Someone from the school dropped us off in Vienna, and from there we took the train home together, just a few days after Dad's birthday, on August twenty-sixth.

Had anyone noticed that Dad was not looking forward to his birthday so much as dreading it—a typically dismal assessment on his part—I'm sure it could have been arranged for us to come home a few days earlier. But that never occurred to anyone. We children would have welcomed the free time before school started, although if we had been forced to come back for Dad's birthday, I can imagine how we would have gone on about not being able to finish together with everyone else.

No one was paying enough attention to realize how much Dad's sixtieth birthday meant to him, how badly he wanted to be alone with just his wife and children, and how unhappy it made him to receive visits from friends and relatives instead.

Mom could sense that this birthday mattered to Dad, but she was trying so hard to make it nice for him that she forgot how different her own birthday parties were—which was exactly the kind that Dad wanted. She also forgot that we had always respected Grandpa's wishes for no presents or guests, just a gathering of the extended family.

It was the twenty-sixth of August, the day the Czech king Přemysl Otakar II fell in the Battle of Austerlitz (not that our dad felt any special affinity with Otakar; he knew at least a dozen other tragic events that had happened on St. Rufus Day, that's simply the only one I remember). And when at last that hectic, unfortunate day had come to a close, our dad sat in his bedroom alone, looking back on his life, and right then and there he made up his mind: "If I'm alone, I'm alone. I'm too old to lie to myself anymore!"

The explosion had been building up inside him since breakfast, gaining force throughout the exhausting day of visits, congratulations, and general merriment. As his feeling of isolation grew, he could only catch fragments of the goings-on around him. He wasn't part of it, and kept slipping off into his own gloomy world, where he completely forgot that his wife was seriously ill—especially since, in the depths of his soul, he saw her sickness as just one more way for her to avoid him. He forgot that she was supposed to depart for the tuberculosis sanatorium first thing in the morning, without even waiting for her children to return from abroad, and that the only reason she hadn't left sooner was because of his birthday party, which she had organized from bed; and that on that day she had risen from bed to eat lunch with him, but had to return to bed to rest several times during the afternoon in order to save herself for that evening. And so he kept searching the party for her—and he was running a fever again, it was so hot and muggy—but someone had said that Eliška had a fever, too—and he just kept on searching and searching.

So after a sleepless night of thinking the whole thing through, he burst into his sick wife's bedroom at five in the morning to announce that he couldn't go on living this way, he wanted a divorce. ("What could he possibly have been lacking?" Aunt Blažena asked afterward.) He told her to leave and to take all of the children with her. Living on his own couldn't be any worse. To all of this, our startled mother, now wide awake, silently agreed with a nod.

Mom didn't write us about her illness because she hadn't wanted to upset us while we were abroad. But following this unexpected turn of events, she wanted to talk to us as soon as possible. Exhausted and distraught after first the birthday party and then Dad's announcement on top of it, she consented to let Grandma send us a telegram, provided she didn't mention the divorce. All four of us received the same message: *Mom in sanatorium. Wants to see you.* We would have been alarmed to hear that she was sick and in the sanatorium regardless. But the fact that our normally unruf-fled mom hadn't written us herself, and that Dad hadn't written either, started us thinking the worst.

When we arrived, we were more reassured by Mom than by Dad, who didn't seem to know what to say. We phoned her right away at the sanatorium and promised to come the next morning.

We then spent an unusually pleasant evening with Dad. It was as though this single crisis had swept aside everything trivial that had come between us over the years; all of us were with Mom in our thoughts, and the only reason we didn't talk about her was to avoid feeding our anxiety. Usually after supper we would all just get up and go off to do our own thing—unless we were ordered to stay, in which case we moved into the study or the sunroom for coffee and dessert, and then stayed there reading newspapers and mag-azines and listening to records until we were given permis-sion to leave. But this time we all remained seated at the table, basking in the feeling of being a family.

Ordinarily when we ate in the big dining room, we turned on all the lights plus the chandelier over the table, since otherwise it would depress Dad to see the dark room behind us. But this time, once the table had been cleared, Dad asked the maid to switch off the other lights. I can remember sitting around the table, with flowers in the cen-ter ("Not too tall," Dad always said, "so you can see the per-son across from you"), sipping tea and nibbling cookies. As the warm circle of light shone down on us, it contrasted cozily with the darkened room beyond its borders, height-ening the feeling of togetherness. And as the garden's sweet summer smells drifted in through the big open window, for once Dad was not "haunted by its blackness"—as he had been known to say before ordering the window closed and the curtains drawn.

Dad himself didn't talk much, although he asked a lot of questions and actually listened as we each talked over the others in our rush to tell our story first. Despite our excitement, we kept our voices low so as to avoid disturbing the ailing mother who was there with us in our thoughts. We told him all about what we had done and what it was like, and he didn't interrupt even once with his usual "You know, when I was your age . . ." We could see that he wasn't all there, even though he listened and nodded his head, but given the situation, his agitation seemed natural.

Which made us all the more stunned, insulted, and angry the next day when Mom told us that he had asked for a divorce.

"He's the one who's such a pain, and Mom is the one who suffers for it!"

"I can't believe this is happening!"

"Who else would do a thing like that at a time like this?"

"The arrogance!"

"How could he look us in the eye last night?"

"The coward didn't even drop a hint."

"He didn't dare—as usual, we had to hear it from Mom."

"His typical perfect timing, ha ha ha!"

"Come on, forget it. It happened and that's all that counts. You yourself never would have had the nerve to ask for a divorce, Mom. At least now we'll have some peace and quiet."

The boys were furious at first, but just a few minutes later they were giggling with excitement and making plans for their new life. Libuše and I held out a long time before bursting into tears, telling ourselves that divorce was the best thing for everybody. I have a foggy memory of Mom, dark circles under her eyes, biting her lip, a baffled, dumbstruck little girl, her weary head standing out darkly against the white pillowcase.

Even though our parents never went to church or adhered to any religious precepts, they considered the act of matrimony and the creation of a family to be a natural tie binding them together for as long as they lived. They accepted their marriage the way some parents accept it when their child is born with a birth defect; it was their destiny. Even if the thought of divorce had crossed their minds in times of difficulty, they had never seriously considered it.

And now, suddenly, the possibility presented itself. Emancipation beckoned, and even then, Mom didn't seize the initiative. It was up to us children to set the matter in motion.

We got in late from visiting Mom, we were still in bed the next morning when Dad had breakfast, and by lunchtime we were out of the house. We moved into our grandfather's place, feeling no obligation to say anything after the way Dad had ignored us when we came home the night before—we disappeared without a word.

I wonder what he thought it meant?

How long did it take him to realize that we had deserted him—our own father? What did he think when that first lunch came and went with no sign of us? Normally when one of us couldn't make it, we would call him up or leave a note. I wonder if he asked around about us. He was probably too embarrassed. And who would he have asked, anyway? I wonder what he thought at dinner that day, and at lunch the next, and every day after—and Sundays, when he didn't even have his work to take his mind off of it. How long did he wait for a phone call or a letter?

The funny thing was, we weren't the only ones who were incapable of thinking straight. Everyone was appalled, they all shook their heads in disbelief that our dad was capable of such a thing. But no one, not a single person, went to him and said, "Listen to me, Matouš. I'm sure you didn't really mean it, so just take it back, at least until Eliška gets better. Then you can see." No one said anything.

Of course our parents were both too discreet to give anyone the chance. Our mom's relatives felt somehow tainted by the whole business, and tried to hide it, though it was obvious from the way they tiptoed around us. As for Dad's side, no one in his family had ever gotten divorced, and they considered it a disgrace. All of our parents' closest friends had figured out that it wasn't easy for Eliška being with a volatile husband like Matouš, but that was all they knew, and they were stunned to the point of speechlessness.

And so suddenly our dad found himself alone on an island in the midst of a storm that he himself had unwittingly unleashed, utterly defenseless and unable to explain to anyone that they were condemning him unjustly. It wasn't he who had stampeded the horses, they had run away with him, foaming at the mouth with blood, their fiery hooves racing over the stones. He had been carried off like Smolíček, the little boy of legend, taken hostage by witches and dragged along the ground, through thorns and brambles. . . .

And in that moment of crisis, Dad's favorite sister turned to her son: "Why don't you take your uncle under your wing? I'm at my wits' end, and he's so miserable." The foolish Karel-Charles of course interpreted his mother's request in his own way: He invited Dad out to dinner and brought along a young lady who wasted no time in taking care of the dignified industrialist. The phrase "taking care of" comes from Charles, who later confessed to the whole thing. According to him, Dad didn't like to be left alone with the young lady, so whenever they went to dinner Charles had to come along. Chattering away, the young lady would stroke Dad's cheek and every now and then naughtily peck at the food on his plate (by the time it reached us, the story was that they shared a plate); sometimes she would even lay her head on his shoulder. They were only together without Charles there once, when the young lady came up with the idea of taking a trip to the country. As they were entering the town of Borová, however, Dad drove off the road and ran into a willow tree right next to the river. His lady companion fled the scene in panic and never bothered him again. So much for Dad's distraction.

He was probably too ashamed to go to any of the lawyers he knew, which means the lawyer who filed the divorce suit against our mother—our mom being sued!—was quite likely an acquaintance of the young lady's.

Still, it is worth noting that the suit wasn't filed until six months after Dad had announced his decision—six months without a single word from his wife and children, living all alone in that big deserted house, walking the expansive garden by himself, night after night. It was as if he had challenged himself to a duel that he no longer wanted and yet there was nothing he could do. His distant family's silence goaded him: "What are you waiting for? Just go ahead and do what you said you would!"

It would be pointless to add that events raced unstoppably ahead to their tragic conclusion. That, at least, is the way I would have put it back then, but today I would ask: Where is the end and where is the beginning?

It only seems strange that Dad didn't decide to kill himself sooner—although, as we know, people can bear much more than we think, more than even they themselves realize.

And yet, had it not been for Mom's illness and had she been at home, then even if we had gone on avoiding him, speaking icily to him, if at all, with Mom maintaining her typical silence, our attitude might have served to dampen his mood swings. Add to that the effect of Libuše's tears and mine, and Dad might have moved from a state of adolescent defiance into one of deep depression. Then, of course, we would have felt sorry for him again, all talk of divorce would have ceased, and everything would have fallen back into the same old routine, in which no one really understood anyone, not even themselves. But none of that happened.

On the first page of one of his dream journals, Dad had written, "God calls on us without knocking (a Russian proverb)."

Eldergent had no idea how much help he was in extracting this painful confession. I don't recall his interrupting me with a single word or comment. He just sat and sat. But his sympathy and understanding flowed freely. At one point in my story, he rose from his chair with his usual difficulty, pulled up a stool, and sat down beside me, doubled over, head in his hands. When I finished, I realized that he was holding both my hands. The two of us were silent for quite a while; I knew what he was saying to me in his mind, and he knew what I was answering. Then he saw me to the door, and when he spoke, his quiet voice seemed to be the natural continuation of our conversation rather than an interruption of the long silence:

"Well, there's no point in dredging up those painful memories anymore now, is there?"

I looked at him in surprise and thought: If only he were right. But since I didn't yet dare to believe it, I just smiled feebly. Eldergent smiled back, and said with ever-so-gentle emphasis:

"I clearly remember you saying that your father changed tremendously at the end of his life and none of you even noticed."

I stood there dumbstruck, utterly numb from head to toe.

"And after nearly twenty years, he wrote to his children: 'If I wasn't able to serve as a good example, then at least let me stand as a warning.'"

Feeling all of a sudden as if I had inhaled an invigorating breath of fresh air, I added jubilantly:

"Why yes, yes he did, when he was in the home, lying on one side of him was an old farmer who had been afraid of retirement all his life, and on the other side was a butler who had been afraid what would become of him when he turned old and sick, and they were both so delighted to have a clean bed in a warm room with regular meals, and thankful for the way their lives had turned out. Yes, yes," I was breathless with excitement. "And Dad wrote: 'I am all the worse off now for having had it so good before.' So he did change. He actually changed a great deal!"

"And his children did too," Eldergent added solemnly. And I said to myself: Let psychologists declare, with a dismissive wave of the hand, that human nature cannot be changed. And yet they haven't an inkling about the actual makeup of us poor mortals, whose true self lies buried beneath layers of mournful sediment.

O Lord, dear Lord, the rules may be different from the ones in fairy tales, but grown-up life still has its share of dazzling miracles.

Then suddenly I felt something happening inside me, deep down at the very core, as if things were being rearranged and uncovered, who knows?

I was still standing in the doorway, ready to leave, my hand on the doorknob, but part of me was back in that long-ago time before I was born, with Mom in her white dress, hair flowing down, standing one foot on the terrace as Dad waited for her; and simultaneously I was off in some faraway place where everything existed on a higher plane, free of pain, where there was neither room nor reason for injury, injustice, malice, or misunderstanding, where everything was just *different*. Only the slenderest of threads connected the person standing at Eldergent's door to the one out there, and yet each of them was equally real and compelling. But now, right now, is my time here, here in this world where people are born, spend their lives in toil, and die, guided throughout by the beacon of hope.

The doorknob is warm from my hand, I feel my right shoulder leaning against the closet by the door, and wrinkle by wrinkle, taking my time, I study the furrowed map of the smiling Eldergent's eighty-five-year-old face—through a fissure of an instant I touch him too in the time before he was and will be no longer—and then I am back at the door with my hand on the doorknob, and the two of us are smiling at each other like two scheming little children who have discovered something in the attic but refuse to talk about it, even among themselves.

A feeling wells up in me, silky and soft. At first I resist. Now don't deceive yourself, I think, but then I have to admit to myself that it's real, I can feel it: The shackles have been released, the pressure from so long ago has ceased. I am free.

It's strange the way sometimes thoughts pile up inside your head, stacked one on top of the next, and just sit there, still as a courtroom before a hearing, and your head is so crowded it's ready to burst. Then at other times they get impatient and start talking back and forth to each other, which for thoughts means movement, and the next thing you know your head is spinning. And then again, every so often a thought comes along that fills your head up all by itself, digging itself in nice and good. Idle one moment, laboring frantically the next, it either runs you straight into the ground or leads you to a triumphant breakthrough.

When I was in Kladruby for physical therapy, I met a bricklayer who spent three weeks telling me everything that had passed through his mind in the few seconds before he hit the ground after falling off his scaffolding. He said that some thoughts and memories had flown through him in flocks and throngs, while others came to him individually. "I'm telling you, lady, it was a miracle. I started going over it all again as soon as I came to in the hospital. I got so carried away, I didn't even think to ask what had happened to me until a couple days later. It didn't even seem that important at first when I figured out that I couldn't move. I was too busy thinking about what I saw when I fell."

line. But she chose not to ask any questions, and hurried the boy into bed so the two of them could be alone.

As Libuše walked out of the bedroom, Dad motioned to her, "Have a seat." He then proceeded to tell her how that afternoon he and David had been building a small fire at Kinsky Gardens, up on the hill near the wall at the back of the park, where usually no one went, when a groundskeeper had come up and started to yell at them.

Libuše was so stunned she couldn't contain herself, shrieking, "You mean that you—" Before she could finish her sentence, Dad dismissed her with a cavalier wave of his hand, proclaiming:

"You should have heard the way David stood up for me! He took a step forward, even though he was afraid, and said: 'We'll pay the fine, but that doesn't give you the right to shout at Grandpa!'"

This time Libuše didn't write. She called me up on the phone that same evening, after Dad had left. As she gave me the report on what had happened, I could hear her voice trembling with joy, spilling over with emotion, but couldn't bring myself to do anything more than thank her over and over again for calling. I hung up the phone and just sat there for a long time with tears streaming down my face, and in my mind I could picture Old Valenta's children loading their drunken pop onto the wheelbarrow—and the four of us, standing on the other side of the path, suddenly go racing over to Dad, as he falls, gently, slowly, the way it always is in dreams.

Whenever I cooked supper at Eldergent's place, I tried to make enough so he would have leftovers the next day. But that night, we were both in such a fabulous mood that we were positively glowing, and the spaghetti tasted so good to us, we ate it all. Then suddenly I recalled yet another good thing about our father, perhaps even better than the time when David saved him from the lion's den. "Dad's illegal activities" was the way we referred to it whenever it came up, although it was quickly forgotten when hard times set in for us all. Mojmír left the country, Mom passed away, Petr and Libuše went to prison, I was in the sanatorium with spinal tuberculosis, my children went to stay with Aunt Beatrice, and David—can you believe it? I don't even know how—ended up in a boardinghouse. It was too much all at once, one thing stacked on top of the next—the kind of situation you couldn't invent if you tried, if you know what I mean—and the next thing we knew, we were separated by all sorts of endless distances, as in some fevered nightmare.

Years later, after David was grown up and living in London, Libuše showed me a letter he had written that she found among Dad's papers. It was dated 12/5/51, which meant it came from the time when David was in the boardinghouse and his parents were in prison. "Will you look at how well those two got along?" Libuše said.

"Dear Grandpa, I think about you all the time. How are you, what are you doing? Alone, alone, alone, and alone again. Hugs and kisses, your David."

Next to David's signature, written in Dad's hand, was: Eleven years old.

But not to forget Dad's illegal activities.

"You wouldn't know someone who lives alone, doesn't get many visitors, and is 100 percent reliable, would you?" It was a few days after the "February Revolution," in 1948, when I ran into an old childhood friend of mine on Národní Avenue.

"Why of course: our dad!"

"You think so?" my friend drawled hesitantly. He was trying to fish our confounded family history out of his memory, I could read it right from his nose. "Actually, you're right. Your family has been through a lot, so I suppose you would understand these things. . . . Oh my God, I'm sorry. My mind is so all over the place, I didn't even realize I was thinking out loud. What I meant was, if you think it will work, that would be fantastic. We would be extremely grateful."

"Just forget it. What do you need?"

"I'm ashamed, and afraid you'll be offended. Just think it over, though, and if you accept, then ask your father if he could take in a lady who needs to hide away for a while, just a week or so. She's very sweet and easy to get along with. She would be quiet as a mouse and wouldn't get in the way. It's my father's lady friend."

So the minister has such worries even in these stormy times? I thought. Now it was my friend's turn to read my forehead, and he said:

"It's not just for him; it's for my mother, my sisters—everyone."

Dad said yes of course. He was delighted to be of use to someone. By that point, he had been living on his own for over ten years, and he was painfully unhappy. His friend Cyril had tried to convince him that his failed suicide was an act of Providence, but Dad saw things differently. He was angry at God, and rebuked Him often for not understanding, for deeming Dad worse than he actually was, and therefore keeping him here in this world instead of sending him a nice, comfortable death.

That summer, when Libuše reminded him to get coal for the winter, he raged until the glass in the cabinet rattled: "What wickedness have I done that I deserve to live through another winter?" Then, however, his heart seized up so fiercely that they both thought it was the end, and when it turned out not to be, they felt foolish.

The only solace our Dad had were the dreams he so painstakingly recorded in his journals upon awakening, and his "mysticism."

But even then, he never entirely forgot that he was a chemist, and continued with his experiments. The kitchen stove and shelves were covered with vials, flasks, and all sorts of mysterious powder-filled vessels. His research, however, extended beyond chemistry to the culinary arts as well. He liked to boast that he had never owned or read a single cookbook—and it was true: Boiled, baked, or fried, everything he made was of his own invention. None of us would admit it, but sometimes the results were superb.

One day Dad discovered a lovely green lawn sprouting in a dish of forgotten lentils. Delighted at the happy fluke that had caused grass to grow in the midst of freezing temperatures and calamitous snowstorms, he interpreted it as a greeting from friendly spirits. We only chuckled at his housekeeping practices, and were always glad once we had made our way out again through the clutter of pots, bottles, and vials to reach fresh air.

In the middle of our dad's chemistry lab–cum–culinary workshop stood a boarded-over bed which the cook had once slept on, and across the entrance hall was the large and still-elegant bedroom. Dad approvingly referred to it as the cheerful room, although in fact the part that held his enormous bed, curtained off by an Aubusson tapestry, was rather spooky. What gave the room its cheerful quality was the bay window: nice and spacious and sunny and full of flowers. Unfortunately there was no canary or parakeet, which I will blame myself for until the day I die, because although now I realize how much Dad loved birds, at the time we never had any idea what to give him for Christmas—it never occurred to us.

Dad offered the minister's lady friend his room, but declining his chivalry with a thousand thanks she modestly settled herself in the kitchen. Ever since the cook left because she couldn't adjust to Dad's way of life, he had been constantly reminding us that he had two vacancies for sleeping, so he was open to overnight guests. No one ever took him up on it, though. Except of course David, who adored his visits to Grandpa's. Everything there was so exciting: the sorcerer's kitchen, the gigantic bed with the tapestry curtain he would open and close the whole time he was visiting. Whenever this got on Libuše's nerves, Dad would assure her,

"Why, he isn't doing anything wrong," and David would go right on opening and closing, gazing earnestly up at his grandpa. Some of the other attractions were a music box with metal keys, a toolbox—complete with hammer, pliers, screwdrivers, drills, and saw—and undoubtedly plenty of other magical objects that none of us was aware of.

Dad and David went to bed at midnight and took their midday meal at three in the afternoon; everything, in short, was different from the way it was for David at home. That was a given, and Libuše had resigned herself to it once every so often. What was worse was that Dad's apartment had bedbugs. It was the cleaning lady who discovered them. Dad said he hadn't noticed them, but that in any case they were God's creatures too. As for the rest of us, we never did get over our shock, though we had to admit that any bedbugs of Dad's had to be truly special. Whenever we visited his apartment, we would go straight over to Libuše's afterward and climb into the empty bathtub (that was Mojmír's idea), where we would then carefully undress, scrupulously examining each piece of clothing. Even after that, the cook and the maid, frantic at the thought of the bedbugs spreading, would thoroughly inspect every layer. Strangely enough, though, we never found a single one.

But to return to Dad's illegal activities.

A few days after the lady moved in, Dad turned up at our place. Sporting an immaculate haircut, he was freshly shaven, with an impeccable suit and an expensive fur coat that I hadn't seen on him in ages. I was angry and confused. I remembered all of the times that I had dressed up in my latest finery, the baby stylishly resplendent in his smart white carriage, and Dad came to meet us in the park wearing cheap woolen shoes, an old pair of hand-hemmed ski pants, and a short fur coat that Mom had set aside years ago for walks in the woods. And now here he was, once again the polished gentleman, looking like Emil Jannings in the role of a White Army general.

Naturally the lady boarder was charming, modest, delightful, sweet. She understood and accepted everything. I was furious. What exactly did she understand? That nonsense Dad had been feeding her about Mom? Of course he was unloading himself. All those years with no one to talk to, and now an opportunity like this! And God forbid that a lady in her situation wouldn't be modest! She had been advised of the bedbugs at Dad's place, and if even that didn't bother her, she must really be in a jam.

"What about the critters?" I asked Dad. "Doesn't the lady mind?" But he just smiled happily, not a cloud darkening his face. I think I could count the number of times I had seen him smile like that.

"We even get along when it comes to that—can you imagine?" He spoke slowly and emphatically. "The bedbugs don't go after her either, so actually we (we!) don't mind. She's a wonderful woman, you know. You must come by and meet her. Even you would like her, I'm sure of it."

The stress on the word *you* was intended to mean "even you, who takes after your mother and who therefore inherently, categorically, never likes the same things as I do." Because he was right—because I did take after Mom and got upset when he was cruel to her, and because I loved Mom and not him (or at least so I thought) and it took me a good fifteen years to understand him—I never went over to meet his lady boarder, and I will regret it as long as I live.

As Father Jiří would say, it must have been quite a graceful meeting: Dad in despair, a nuisance to himself and everyone around him, with a woman of roughly forty, who had lost her husband and a child during the war, and had probably just begun to live again when everything happened. And all of a sudden she risked not only imprisonment (God knows why), but having her name tastelessly dragged through the newspapers. From what Dad told me, I believe she was a serious, genuine person—I believe it now, that is—but she sure did make things hard for herself, falling in love with a married man. We all know how touching a man can be when he's dissatisfied with his wife, whether he crassly rails against her or discreetly holds his tongue. And of course loving women trust these men, they feel sorry for them: the poor things, forced to live with wives who don't understand them, alone in a twosome. But at the first sign of crisis, the extramarital woman is tossed overboard. Or not even. That would imply the man cared one way or the other, when most of the time the woman is simply ignored in the crush of other concerns. "We'd better do something about that blasted what's-her-name, or there's going to be trouble. What do you mean for who? Why, for the minister of course." And they hide her away at some sweet old grandpa's.

Positively thrilled to be of use to someone again, the lonely man does what he can. He buys pork and chicken, salads and fruit, and of course flowers and chocolates (he still remembers that one gives chocolates and flowers to ladies), and so the poor woman won't be completely cut off from the outside world, he buys newspapers, too. Every one he can find. He himself hasn't read a paper for years, and has yet to fully grasp what has happened, but he brings the newspapers home to the lady so that she can stay informed.

So one day Dad came home with the papers, a bouquet of violets, and a box of chocolates, set it all down on the kitchen table, and went into his room so as not to disturb her. And as he began watering the plants in the bay window—whenever I remember that window, I see the spot on the wall where the birdcage should have been, and then I think of how we might have found him a dog or a cat or an aquarium full of fish, because Nature is the greatest solace, Dad always said so, and in fact as his age grew, so did his love for all things that live and grow, and surely a few living creatures would have comforted him in his cruel loneliness—and so as he began to water the plants in the window, suddenly he heard a strange sound, like sobbing, coming from the kitchen. Could it be? He heard and felt a tangible, definitely menacing silence. Not a sound, just utter silence. Racing across the hall, he burst in without waiting for her affable invitation—"Please, do come in"—then stopped dead in his tracks. The lady was sitting in a chair, limp and white as a puppet, sobbing on the inside, dry-eyed and mute.

The older gentleman asked no questions, nor did he make any attempt to find out what was wrong; he just stroked her soothingly like a little girl. Then he lifted her up, gently led her into his room, and settled her down in an armchair—the big, soft wing chair that stood next to our fireplace until the family disaster and then followed Dad to Prague, moving with him to his first, second, and third apartment. And each time Dad sat down in it again for the first time after moving, he would say, "I truly hope that this is the last waiting room, because I'm not going anywhere else from here." But of course he did, because those were revolutionary times. After he died, the chair went to Petr's blind grandmother, and a few months later, when she was digging around in it, she discovered a box of English tea with a label in Dad's handwriting: *Greetings from London, from a precious guest.*

This is how it happened: I was out in the springtime sun, pushing the baby carriage in front of the museum in Kinsky Gardens. The baby was asleep, so I was just glancing around and going over my English vocabulary. Suddenly, all the way down the path, at the bottom of the hill, I spotted a cluster of people with Dad's profile towering over them. From that distance, I couldn't see anything but his shoulders, the tilt of his head, and the rhythm of his gait—but it was enough for me to recognize that it was him and that the lady had left.

The closer he came, the more apparent it was: something momentous had happened; he was coming as a messenger. It wasn't that he looked sad as he made his way up the hill. In fact he appeared to be neither downhearted nor cheerful. No matter how I racked my brains, I couldn't describe him. Not because I was too lazy, but all at once I didn't dare to judge him. I felt esteem and respect, as if he were someone else, or in fact just the opposite, as if he were . . . Suddenly, as he took his last few steps toward me, I saw a different man than the one I was accustomed to: not the source of all the family's troubles, an often disagreeable crank, but the person underneath it all. I recall the thought flashing through my mind: This must be the way God, who understands him, sees him. It's hard to believe but true. This moment actually happened; in the space of a few seconds, I saw more than I had in years of struggling to understand—and then the flash of truth was forgotten. I don't understand it, but I do know it happened.

"She ought to be in London by now," he said quietly.

If only I had said aloud what was going through my head! "You mean the lady who respects, appreciates, and admires you, who felt good when she was around you—the woman who made you the changed man that you are now."

The poor woman had gone into shock after reading in the newspaper that a certain minister's lady friend had jumped out the top-floor window of a hotel. All she could do was point to the article, speechless. But Dad had failed to understand, and innocently tried to comfort her—he was actually laughing, he told me—"Why that's ridiculous, you're right here with me. Nothing has happened to you, and nothing is going to. Why, you wouldn't jump out a window." And only then did her tears start to flow, which means he was of some help, after all. Once she had recovered her voice, she explained to him that she had thought she was the minister's only lover.

When Dad finished the story, he said: "We had some unforgettable moments together. Both difficult and uplifting." Doubtless there had been other occasions when he would have liked to reminisce about her with me, but unfortunately he had a stupid daughter, and so he preferred to keep his thoughts to himself. For the same reason, he also didn't tell me when a certain someone brought him greetings from London. Or maybe he did, but it mattered so little to me that I forgot about it.

Perhaps he had kept that box of tea on the shelf by his bed for some time, next to the watch that hung under the shelf. And one day, lost in thought, he had held the box in his hand and settled into his armchair—there they were, the two of them, strolling through Hyde Park, when they saw two lawn chairs folded up on the grass beneath the shade of the venerable elms. Well, they would just sit right down and have themselves a chat. But as he was opening up the lawn chairs, he dropped the box of tea, and it slipped beneath the seat cushion.

Then they drove him to the hospital—and again he had to move—and again he was in the hospital—and then he ended up in the home.

David hitchhiked over from the boardinghouse to visit him a few times, and told us the old people from the home said that Dad looked like President Masaryk. Václav operated a bulldozer nearby, so he went to see Dad as well. No one else could make the trip. Václav said he thought it was the tall frame and goatee, quite unusual for the time, that reminded the old folks of Masaryk. But I think they could also sense that special dignity which we failed to perceive. That something which I had glimpsed for a moment and then forgotten: the gift of self-confidence given him by that lady.

Dream journal no. 119, 1955, six months before his death.

I am dead. My body has already departed, and while my mind—or is it my soul? I no longer wish to deceive myself—has yet to leave me, it is no longer at one with my body. It has begun to slip away, and soon it will be released. This is the moment of uncoupling into lifeless body and the rest, now perceiving and observing.

The weather is hot, so the arrangements for disposing of my body must be made quickly.

There are people present—no one close to me—making conversation and telephone calls in the next room. The talk on the phone especially intrigues me; I hear and feel the voices meeting over the airwaves. Just as I am starting to grasp things in a new way, there is an interruption. Live people undress me, discussing something that does not concern me, lifting my arm, my leg. They load me in and carry me off somewhere—probably to the autopsy. If I were to see all of this while I was alive, I know that I would be amazed at all sorts of things, but whatever it is that has slipped away from my body—I would no longer call it mind, soul, or spirit, but perhaps my bare, fundamental self—acts as a disinterested observer, documenting the scene in an utterly impersonal fashion. My perception is, however, many times greater than ever before. As if I had countless eyes and ears, thousands of sensory organs. If I were to write out all that my self observed in that brief time, what a tremendous book it would make.

Among other things, I have a record of each particular of my dead body, as well as of those who were handling it, standing around me, approaching and receding. Every color, texture, and shade of the body of the dead and the bodies of the living. The way the color of their clothing, for instance, shifted almost imperceptibly as the material came into contact with my dead body; the way the color, shade, and temperature altered in the atmosphere enclosing my dead body and the bodies of the living.

All of this my bare self observed with the calmness of a cool light.

Once the work on my body was finished and everyone left, my soul was able to breathe deeply and have a look around—funny that now I'm inclined to say soul—*and only then did true sight, entirely different from what I had just experienced, spread out before me. Unfortunately, only for an instant and then I awoke.*

I believe that in this dream—if it was a dream—I overtook my fast-approaching future.

I don't know who brought it up. But all at once we started to talk about how it was high time to give Dad a proper burial. None of us thought it appropriate that his urn was hidden away in a vault with his sister, our Aunt Anna, and her son, the ill-fated Charles, without any plaque or inscription because it was considered temporary. And yet for more than ten years, we were incapable—incapable, incapable—it would have been hard for us to explain, but we simply failed to do anything one way or the other: Not only was Dad's last wish—to be scattered over Blue Mountain—not honored, but he didn't even get a little nameplate in the vault with Aunt Anna, as Libuše and I had suggested. Václav had said we would do it when Mojmír returned from exile. But as the years flew by, all of us, including Václav, realized that he was gone for good. Then we agreed we would do it as soon as he came to visit, so we could all be together. And still he didn't come. It's unbelievable, really, quite insane—something like that could only happen in our family.

And then suddenly, in '68, before the Soviet army invaded, Mojmír wrote: "Make whatever arrangements are necessary for us to bury Dad as he wished. A year from now I probably won't be able to get through anymore."

Quickly Libuše, Václav, and I pulled ourselves together. The first thing we did was make a trip to the cemetery for Václav to dig up the urn in secret. Because, as it turned out, getting a permit to scatter ashes on Blue Mountain was impossible.

Václav insisted that it would be easy, and that early in the morning no one would be there. But as he was digging the second hole—he had been present when the urn was laid in the ground, and said that he made a point of having it placed just beneath the surface and remembered where—just as all three of us were beginning to worry that he wouldn't find it, or that it had been stolen, we noticed an old lady heading unswervingly our way. Before we could figure out what to do, she greeted us cheerfully, explaining that she just had to point out that this wasn't the best time of year to be planting rhododendrons. Luckily we had listened to Libuše and brought a rhododendron plant along with the spade and the rake. The old lady went on and on about how she came to the cemetery every day and loved to chat with everyone she met. After a while I had developed a headache and Václav's forehead was streaming sweat—partly from the digging, but also because of the lady. At last he said, rather rudely: "Didn't you come to see someone?" The old lady got the message and walked off without a word. We all felt sorry for her, but it probably was the only way to get the poor woman to leave us alone. Then, as Václav went back to digging, Libuše and I stood there bulging our eyes at each other, silently flapping our mouths open and closed like fish. It was a sort of childhood game that we used to play whenever we felt dazed and helpless.

"Hand me that bag and the rhododendron," Václav called out softly, and before we knew it, the deed was done.

Sneaking around with your dad's urn in a plastic bag, that is one thing you never forget! There were moments when it felt as though Dad were there walking next to us, just like the old days. With one step, we were little children again, the smallest ones hoisting their hands high to his, as we merrily trotted along, gabbing away among ourselves; with the next, we were scowling grown-ups, hanging our heads, no one saying a word; and with the next step, and the next; and as we walked, it seemed as though we could feel our dad, unbecomingly shrunken and huddled inside the shopping bag, and it was a horrible feeling—and on and on, back and forth, the way it is in those situations, one minute your throat is choked and you've got chills up and down your spine, the next you feel like laughing hysterically and it takes all the self-control you can muster to continue walking in silence.

As Václav laid the bag with the urn on the backseat of the car, we all stood there gaping, as though we couldn't figure out how it got there. Then Libuše climbed in, taking the bag on her lap like a child, and as one great big tear rolled down her cheek and onto the bulky package, the absurdity of it seemed smaller and things began to fall back into a normal human pattern.

My friendship with Eldergent had developed to the point where I was incapable of reliving events without him. Just as I used to phone my mother the minute anything important happened, spitting out the words so fast that I choked on them, now I couldn't bear to wait until I returned to Prague, and called him twice to bring him up to date.

After my return on Friday evening, I went to see Eldergent the next morning, and we agreed to devote the rest of the day to undisturbed conversation. I gave him a hug and put in a quick remark about how well he looked—"as though you had just returned from a good pilgrimage your-self"—before plunging into my story.

"I know that everything I'm about to tell you actually happened," I began, "but still it amazes me. Right now it's all just floating around on the surface, but I know that once it sinks in, it will be completely unchanged and valid.

"As by now you realize, what we had failed to do for more than ten years, we suddenly managed in just a few days. I think that all of us were stunned, although no one said a thing. Not even when Mojmír flew in from Canada and we all met in O. After waiting two days for good weath-er, we made a phone call to Pepík Stloukalů, a childhood pal of David's who now works as a pilot for the local coopera-tive farm, and told him we were on for that day at noon. Even then, we were still in a daze. I think it felt like a dream to all of us, but rather than talk about it, we preferred to pre-tend that it was nothing out of the ordinary.

"And when, after all those years, we parked the car at the foot of Blue Mountain, in the alders at Ore Creek, we discov-ered to our amazement that it hadn't changed a bit since the days when the Gypsies had camped there and the boys had built dams across the creek. Even when we set out on the familiar journey to the top, we still didn't talk about why we were there, instead reminiscing together about who had done what as children—where we had baked potatoes, where we had roasted apples, which was the steepest run down on skis—and as soon as we could see Ore Creek from above, the boys sat down to argue about when and at which spot who had caught the most crayfish. Libuše and I exchanged winks, and then she said softly, 'There's a lot to see, isn't there?' 'You can say that again, and especially in here!' I said, pointing to my head. After a moment of silence, however, we returned to chatting about nothing in particular.

"There was one thing that really surprised us: Blue Mountain was bigger than we had remembered it. Ordinar-ily, when people return years later to the place of their youth, everything seems smaller: the river, the garden, and so on. But when four middle-aged siblings set off on a hike up a 'hill' that they used to take at a trot for the first half, and then make bets on who would be first to the top, and it never took more than an hour, and when now they have difficulties—this one the leg, that one the heart, the third one high blood pressure, and the fourth one, me, my only problem is that I breathe too slowly—then Blue Mountain takes them by surprise: 'Wow, that is far! And uphill all the way!'

"The views, of course, didn't disappoint. As we climbed higher, we took pleasure in watching the wooded hills spread out in every direction, while down below, the river glistened, the train chugged along, and the villages' red rooftops peeked out cheerfully through the trees. It was all even lovelier than we had remembered; even after all our travels around the globe—from Canada to Lake Baikal (and those are also lovely places)—for us this was still the most beautiful spot on earth.

"Then of course we had to admit that it had been a marvelous idea on Dad's part, and we remembered how he used to say that this was where he felt nearest the Lord—and all of a sudden we all joyfully burst out singing 'What a beautiful sight to see God's world,' a tune dredged up from our school days nearly half a century past.

"Mojmír walked some distance ahead of us the whole way. Not because he was in a hurry; he kept looking back and gazing all around just as we did, but evidently he wanted to be alone with his thoughts. All at once, though, he veered off to the right, took a few steps, and then turned around to see whether we agreed. As soon as he took that first step to the right, we realized that he wanted to make a small detour to stop at the miracle well, and so we waved him on, hollering our consent, as Mojmír turned around again and continued on his way.

"The well lay downhill from a glade of buttercups, in a small dell that was indisputably our parents' most beloved spot. Although they didn't believe in the well's miraculous powers, they said it had probably been a sacred site in pagan times. Dad had had the water tested and it turned out there was nothing unusual about it, other than the fact that it had a slight laxative effect — 'and that can work wonders sometimes!' as Dad put it. For us children, however, the well remained a miracle. We gladly and willingly believed all the tales of those who had been helped by its water, and even invented a few of our own. And of course no one could deny its excellent taste. Whenever we had an especially honored guest, Dad would send one of us to the well, and for anyone he thought would fail to appreciate the delicious water in its pure form, we would brew a pot of tea, and our guests always had to admit that it was the best they had ever tasted.

"The only change that we could see at the secluded site — the locals wouldn't reveal the secret to just anyone — was a sign announcing that the well's majestic sentinels, a cluster of ancient larches with a single oak in the center, had been granted landmark status. This made us happy on two counts: First, the trees were unharmed and would be protected for posterity, and second, our enamored admiration for the spot had been objectively validated. Once we had recovered from our initial amazement — 'My God! I had forgotten how beautiful it was!' — we settled down around the well to contemplate our surroundings in bliss. Communicating only in hushed tones and gestures, we directed one another's attention to all the lovely details we had once known so well, now seeing them new, more beautiful than ever: the tall moss on the boulder overhanging the well to form a protective roof; the forget-me-nots and multitudes of other flowers and plants whose names we had since forgotten; the enormous oak branch that slithered off through the grass along the earth over which we had once raced to and fro. It was incredible that it had endured, that it had lost none of its former beauty, and we were all unspeakably grateful for it.

"'You know, I don't understand,' Mojmír spoke slowly and thoughtfully, head bowed, as he parted the grass with his hand. 'It's been twenty years since I've been here, but I just couldn't come any sooner. All of you, though, you say that you were here once, and you twice . . . ?' he pointed to Václav, then Libuše, then me. We just mutely shook our heads from side to side. Mojmír sat on the other side of the well so that he could see us and we could see him, and the four of us silently conversed for a while. I think that even without words we communicated better than ever before, during any of our conversations late into the night.

"I have no doubt that for each of us there are two experiences that especially stand out in our memory of the pilgrimage to Blue Mountain: the encounter with the deer family, and sitting around the well. These two events possess relevance not only in and of themselves, but as part and parcel of the ash-scattering ceremony (and of course it was a ceremony, even though none of us used that word), embedded in its multilayered totality, once hidden from us but now laid open wide.

"We all made fun of each other, but still we stood up time after time to look at our reflections in the well again and again. Maybe it actually does work miracles, we began to think afterward, because whenever we leaned over the water, we saw not only our middle-aged faces of today, but also the young ones of the past. We couldn't stop looking. With each shift from old to young, a movie flashed through our minds of everything that had happened to us and around us in that interval. It wasn't merely a documentary, but rather a confession shining up through the well's clean, clear water.

"Whether it was all that staring into the well or walking through that gloomy old forest afterward, I don't know, but we started to speak less and less, then only under our breath, until in the end we all fell silent, engrossed in our own thoughts and recollections."

Eldergent followed the entire account with his usual blend of active and unobtrusive concern. At some points he merely let out a satisfied sigh, at others he fervently nodded approval. Then every so often he couldn't hold back and gleefully cried out: "Oh yes, yes, I can picture it as if I were there!" And when I came to a stop and asked, "Doesn't it seem like a bit too much magic to you?" he practically exploded: "No, no, I beg you, go on!"

Every now and then we had to stop to catch our breath, but with each meter we climbed, it felt as though we were leaving behind another piece of the weight and confusion still lingering within us. And with each new panorama that unfurled from the forest's edge, we felt a little bit freer.

"Perhaps the others felt the same way I did; it was as if at a certain point we crossed into another atmosphere. Our parents always said that the air was different once you entered the woods above the buttercup glade. Maybe it really was the air, or maybe it was because all of us were dwelling on Dad in our thoughts; either way, I was suddenly reminded of the moment I was granted to view him at the crematorium.

"I stopped at his open coffin, feeling neither sad nor moved. Most of all, I was surprised to see that he had his own head back, instead of the pitiful little one I had failed to recognize when I visited him in the hospital. The expression on his face was blessedly peaceful and marvelously abstract. It was the same abstract quality that statues of Greek gods possess, conveying the impression of being somewhat removed from all worldly matters. But while their pagan abstraction is entirely devoid of presence, Dad's face was remarkable in that it maintained a presence of sorts. As when halfway between dreaming and waking we hear the children rising for school across the hall, and then breakfast being prepared in the kitchen; we can determine precisely which sound goes with what, as we begin to think of the day's work ahead, yet we are incapable of lifting an eyelid.

"It dawned on me then that the time-honored custom of holding wakes for the dead is more than a mere formality. It took me years to realize many things that, had I been able to remain with my dead father a few hours, I might have arrived at there, in his silent, posthumous proximity, wide open and restful, curiously eloquent, capable of sorting out anything. As it was, in the brief time granted me, I grasped only one thing: that I was face to face with, or rather inside of, something that would not soon, like this body, finish in flames. It felt as though someone had gently peeled away the outermost vestment of my soul. What next? I wondered.

"Now I know. I feel like an old soldier, a bit worse for wear but not dissatisfied, and I think—I believe—that Dad would be pleased.

"At last Mojmír said it for all of us: 'I'm glad that Dad brought us here,' and by *here* we all knew that he meant more than just the place.

"About three hundred meters from the summit, Blue Mountain is completely bare, save for a few stones and patches of dry grass. The oval peak, on the other hand, is blanketed with pines that are stunted and queerly warped from the winds. This peak, which from a distance looked blue, and the bare ring below it were the reason why Dad loved the mountain so much. In summer and winter, again and again, he never failed to be thrilled (nor did we) by the fact that you could circle the entire peak, enjoying a different view in every direction: to one side, the wide river valley; to the other, the deeper and narrower valley carved by the tortuously twisting creek. 'And once you've had enough of standing out in the wind, you can take cover in the woods,' each time he concluded his tribute to the mountain with these words, and he was proud to call it his own.

"Our journey to the top took longer than we had planned, though, so we barely had time to look around and catch our breath before the airplane was overhead. It flew all the way around the bare strip, then made a circle above the peak—we only saw it for a second, since it was hidden by the pines, but we could hear what was happening—then it came back one more time, Pepík waved, made one more loop around the bare circle, and we heard him disappear behind the trees in the direction of Vlkov.

"I didn't watch what anyone else was doing, but I assume that they were all lying on their backs as I was, looking up at the sky for a long time. I would have been happy just to close my eyes and fall asleep on the spot.

"'On your feet, ladies and gents, we're old and our backs are creaky,' Václav declared, standing over me.

"As Libuše raised the kettle of well water over her head and pointed to the mess kit, the rest of us grudgingly had to admit: That Libuše thinks of everything! While the boys began gathering twigs for the fire, she suggested, 'Mojmír and I can get it going'—she probably wanted to talk to him—'you two run off and have another walk around.' By the time Václav and I returned, the first family tea in twenty years with water from the miracle well was ready. Seated on stumps and a length of log, we relished the tea in silence broken only by the occasional murmured 'ahhh' or 'mmm.' We weren't always such quiet campers, in fact most of the time we were almost too chatty; it was only today. There were so many thoughts and feelings flooding from head to head and heart to heart, it would have taken too much time and work to put it all into words. It was better this way. Words seemed to be more suited for humdrum topics, like stamping out the embers, packing up our things, or making a banal joke: 'And being good materialists, we'll remember this too.'

"The wind picked up and it started to get chilly. We knew we had to leave. But none of us wanted to. Instead Libuše and I buttoned up our coats, turned up our collars, and kept on sitting there. And then the second event took place, which brought everything around full circle.

"Suddenly a rustling broke the silence of the murmuring wind; we swung our heads to the right—there was a strong wind blowing from that direction—and there, just a few meters from where we sat, a small family of deer leisurely emerged from the edge of the woods. We were only thinly screened by the sparse bushes, but evidently they were not in the habit of being wary in this area. The deer—I don't know how many there were, I could only sense their immaculate nearness—all stared out at the terrain as if they saw something fascinating. They stood still as statues; only a spark periodically ran through their taut bodies like a charge of electricity, jolting us as well. We didn't even need to think about being quiet. In the blink of an eye, we were frozen solid like the deer, only our gazes were fixed on them instead of into the distance. None of us had ever been so close to wild deer. But the truth is, we failed to make any detailed observations. We were simply drawn into another world, where there was neither will nor wish, only absolute openness and surrender.

"Even after the deer had slowly, glidingly trotted off, we remained motionless for a long time. And it was longer still before we were able to look at one another. Then, gazing back and forth, eye to eye, we said all we needed to say before beginning to make our way back down again. At one point, hearing a few sobs from our dear Libuše, we pulled up short. But then we saw that she was smiling, her tears streaming down unchecked, painlessly washing her clean, so we just nodded gently and continued our slow descent."

Eldergent said nothing, but all of his wrinkles were laughing. What was it about, that smile of his?

The two of us sat there facing each other, looking into each other's eyes, searching them with a smile, until he could no longer contain himself and softly spoke four words. So softly that I didn't understand, and had to lean my ear to his lips, as he repeated: "My daughter is coming."

I took his hand, and yet another distant memory came wafting back.

Libuše's story about the first night after she came home from prison and climbed into David's bed—he was thirteen at the time—and they fell asleep nestled together in the "teddy bear" position. The phrase came from a picture in one of our old, long lost children's books, but all four of us—Mojmír, Václav, Libuše, and I—had committed it to memory forever. At the end of a terrifying adventure, the brown bear and the white bear blissfully fall asleep, the smaller white one snuggling his back up to the brown bear's bosom, safely within his four paws' embrace. Little David of course was the white bear. And as they lay there together without a word, Libuše could feel all the tension and worry that had built up inside her son slowly and quietly draining away, until he was entirely free.

Eldergent spoke: "I began using a different tone in my letters to Dana, then she did the same, and now she's coming." After another silence, he added: "Yes, we have come quite a way."

I didn't so much as stir for a while, then I said: "The Lord calls on us without knocking."

Dream journal no. 82, 1949.

Sometimes I dream that I am a river.

My source lies somewhere in Paradise, and I set out from there on my journey. Nice and easy at first, like a stream. Others perhaps have worries about me, but I myself have none.

Things turn for the worse when, without knowing why, I become a river.

I do not know what to do, or which way to flow. I am pestered by tough soil and all sorts of other obstacles. If I said pestered, I meant it only in jest. I cheerfully stream onward.

I feel the stones rolling along my bottom, I hear the noise as they collide. As rocky ledges loom up defiantly before me, I patiently wear my way under and around them. I squeeze between outcrops, carving narrow ravines for thousands of years, plunging down waterfalls, and then do it all again and again.

Dear gods! Tumbling off the rocky cliff with the full force of my bracing water, I shatter into waves on the boulders below, and as the waves crash back and forth, their frothy white crests spraying high in the air, I rain a foamy shower down upon the trees and ferns along my banks! There are times when I am afraid of the fall, and there are times when I look forward to the tremendous chute down and the antics I will perform when I hit bottom—the mighty roar and the hissing beneath it, followed by a soothing murmur.

And I race on and on. Gathering strength, I push boulders in my path, forming foamy rapids that hurtle upward. In fifty years' time, I will have swept away even that last piece of rock wedged into the overhang.

Sometimes there is nothing to do but flow uphill. Strange, some might even say impossible, but it happened to me more than once. There was no way around it. The water was there, as was the current; what else could I do? And then, though I myself was unaware of it, I had some sort of hidden engines within me; special forces, springs and pistons that compressed and released, propelling my waters upstream.

Atop the ridge, of course, it is glorious. The nearness of the sky, the endless view in every direction, the undulating, wind-driven surge so far removed from all glumness below.

I do not wound or erode these hills, but flow racing over the surface.

I, the river, atop the mountain ridge! After that arduous upward journey—who would ask such a thing of me, how could it have happened, why it's unheard of! Well, so be it, here I am. The music is in me, murmuring, bubbly, flowing and rippling.

Yes, yes, I, the river, atop the mountain ridge.